Rocky jumped down from his seat on the stage. He clenched his fists. (He could do that because, unlike real squirrels, cartoon squirrels have fingers.) Beads of sweat sprang from his forehead as he strained dormant muscles.

I can fly! he told himself. I can fly!

Rocky's tiny gray body began to vibrate.

He pushed himself as never before. . . .

But was it too little, too late?

For just then—high above the stage—Boris Badenov managed to turn on the CDI. "Aha!" the evil fiend cried. "Do I know computers or what?"

Boris aimed the CDI on the biggest target in sight: a six-foot-tall commencement speaker with antlers the width of an exit door.

With his grubby fingers on the computer's mouse, Boris laughed. "With this mouse, I kill Moose."

Could this be the end of Bullwinkle?

SIMON SPOTLIGHT
An imprint of Simon & Schuster Children's Publishing Division
1230 Avenue of the Americas, New York, New York 10020

Manufactured in the United States of America
First Edition   2 4 6 8 10 9 7 5 3 1
ISBN 0-689-82493-9
Library of Congress Catalog Card Number 00-131454

THE ADVENTURES OF ROCKY AND BULLWINKLE THE MOVIE

**Novelization written by
Cathy East Dubowski and Mark Dubowski**

**Based on the motion picture screenplay
written by Kenneth Lonergan**

**Based on characters
developed by Jay Ward**

Simon Spotlight
New York London Toronto Sydney Singapore

CHAPTER 1

The theater was dark. The seats were empty. Not a creature was stirring, not even a moose . . .

And then . . .

A beam of light split the darkness. An old cartoon flickered on the screen. A moose! A squirrel! The famous Rocky and Bullwinkle!

And me, the famous Narrator!

The sound of my voice filled the theater.

In our last episode, our two heroes had set off on a camping trip in the woods outside their hometown of Frostbite Falls, Minnesota. Bullwinkle was just settling down to fish when, suddenly, his two arch-enemies appeared: the villains Boris Badenov and Natasha Fatale. "Don't believe Mr. Narrator!" said Boris with a thick Russian accent. "We are not arch-enemy villains Boris and Natasha! I am Fish and Game Warden Forrest DeSpoiler and she is lovely associate Lotta Chicanery."

"The pleasure is all yours, dollink," said the tall, dark-haired lady by his side.

Then Boris—or Forrest DeSpoiler, as he wished to be called—walked up and gave Bullwinkle a new fishing rod. It was magnetized, and guaranteed to attract fish. Metal fish.

"Is just one problem, Boris," whispered Natasha, or Lotta, as she wished to be called. "Fish are not made of metal."

Immediately DeSpoiler's hand went down and released something in the water. It shot into the current and then stuck onto Bullwinkle's line.

Rocky came to have a look. "Hey, that fish is made of metal," Rocky complained.

"Is steelhead!" Warden DeSpoiler explained.

"But it's put together with nuts and bolts," Rocky said.

"Correction!" the little warden replied. "Is broke trout!"

"Go on," the lady warden told Bullwinkle, "pull the hook!"

"Yeah, pull the hook," said DeSpoiler.

Immediately Bullwinkle's hand went to the hook. Expecting a blast, the wardens reared back, ready to take off. But just as Bullwinkle was about to pull the hook and blow himself and Rocky to smithereens, a force outside their cartoon world stepped in and stopped everything.

The Rocky and Bullwinkle Show was CANCELED!

Rocky, Bullwinkle, Boris, and Natasha froze. "But the cartoon isn't over yet!" they cried.

The cartoon sun went down behind them like a lead balloon, throwing the entire theater into darkness.

"Hey, who turned out the lights?!" Rocky yelled.

They were canceled—for the second time! It was like 1964 all over again—the year *The Rocky and Bullwinkle Show* disappeared from network TV forever. That was the year Boris, Natasha, and Fearless Leader were exiled back to Pottsylvania. And that was the year Rocky and Bullwinkle went home to that bleak and desolate wilderness called RERUNS!

Nearly forty years had passed since that fateful day. Meanwhile, how things had changed! Velcro had replaced the zipper. Sneakers had lights on them. The Cold War was over.

But one thing stayed the same: *The Rocky and Bullwinkle Show* was still canceled!

"But I thought our show was a big hit!" Rocky's voice pleaded in the pitch-black theater, where the old cartoon had finished its run.

No one listened. No one cared—even though the theater where the cartoon had run was located in the heart of Frostbite Falls. The cartoon town was practically deserted. Main Street was boarded up like a ghost town. Dogs slept in the empty streets.

Beyond the city limits, the once-beautiful Frostbite Falls Forest had been reduced to a field of stumps. Every last tree had been cut down by the Slash 'N' Burn Lumber Company.

At nearby Veronica Lake, the once-beautiful waterfall that gave the town its name was choked with pollution from the Consolidated Sludge Corporation.

Most tragically, the famous Narrator from the cartoon show—yours truly—had been reduced to living with his mother, narrating the events of his boring home life.

In the kitchen, I watched as, with speed and dexterity astonishing in a woman of her advancing years, Mother basted the chicken, tossed the salad, and mashed the potatoes.

"OH, SHUT UP!" Mother griped, throwing the saucepan at me.

But perhaps the greatest tragedy of all was playing out in a small cottage in Frostbite Falls's tree-stump area. There, ex-heroes Rocky and Bullwinkle were living out their days on paychecks from reruns of their old show. The checks got smaller and smaller as stations around the world gradually dropped the cartoons.

"Hm. Three and a half cents," Bullwinkle said, reading the amount on his latest check.

Rocky leafed through an old scrapbook. The pages were filled with autographed photos of the stars in their heyday. Newspaper clippings read, "Rocky and Bullwinkle Save U.S.A. Again!" And, "World Leaders Pay Tribute to Rocky and Bullwinkle." And, "Moose and Squirrel—or Gods?"

How things had changed! Now their exploits were only memories. Rocky the Flying Squirrel hadn't flown in years. The pilot's goggles on the leather helmet he wore were clouded with dust.

"What's the point?" the little gray squirrel said to the tall, brown moose. "The world just doesn't need us anymore."

With that, Bullwinkle rose from the couch and headed for the front door.

"Hey! Where are you going?" Rocky said.

Bullwinkle stopped in the open doorway. Beyond him, the stump field stretched as far as the eye could see. "I'm goin' for a walk in the woods," he said with a frown. "All this Chapter One plot setup is wearin' me out!"

CHAPTER 2

Rocky raced out of the house after his friend. "But there aren't any woods anymore, Bullwinkle," he called. "They were all cut down!"

"You don't have to tell me," Bullwinkle replied. The lanky moose turned and stared at the stumps that surrounded them. "I'm the chairman of the Frostbite Falls Society for Wildlife Conversation."

"You mean Wildlife Con-ser-vation," Rocky said.

"What did I say?" Bullwinkle asked.

"You said Wildlife Con-ver-sation."

Bullwinkle frowned. "Well, somebody's gotta start talking about these things!"

Halfway around the cartoon planet from Frostbite Falls, in the cartoon country of Pottsylvania, Rocky and Bullwinkle's sworn enemies—Boris Badenov, Natasha Fatale, and Fearless Leader—were watching over the work of a military firing squad. Pottsylvanians who disagreed with Fearless Leader were standing in line, waiting to be shot.

Suddenly, the Iron Curtain fell.

It landed like a ton of bricks, right on top of the three infamous bad guys and their firing squad. When they heard the crash, a handful of citizens stopped what they were doing, waved limp flags, and said, "Yay," weakly, for freedom. Then they went back to their mindless tasks.

"Dig, you idiots!" Fearless Leader ordered Boris and Natasha. They moaned and tunneled beneath the rubble from the fallen curtain. Fearless Leader's military dress uniform was smudged, and his monocle was askew. Boris was sweating through his black suit. Natasha had broken a fingernail.

Had they known what lay ahead, they would have dug happily. For soon, their efforts in the tunnel would lead them to a new land. A land where the frontier between cartoon and reality is paper-thin. A land where the line drawn in the sand between fact and fantasy has been scrubbed away by the tide. Where, with the right special effects, it might be possible to break through . . . to the other side.

In other words, they were going to Hollywood.

Hollywood, home of Phony Pictures

International and the ambitious but frustrated movie executive Minnie Mogul. She sat at her desk as usual, scanning the title pages of scripts.

"Too stupid," she said about one. "Not stupid enough," she said about another. None of them pleased her.

Suddenly, the TV in her office switched on. She turned to it, amazed to see the cartoon faces of Fearless Leader, Boris, and Natasha staring at her from the screen.

"Hello, Minnie," they all said at once.

"Holy mackerel!" Minnie replied. "Who are you?!"

"Three of the most terrifying villains in the history of children's television," Fearless Leader said proudly.

Boris's smile filled the screen. "How do you do?" he said. He could turn on the charm if he wanted to.

"Nice to meet you," Natasha said sweetly.

But Minnie wasn't fooled. She was Hollywood-tough. "What do you want?" she demanded.

"To do something for you," Fearless Leader replied.

"How would you like to produce *The Rocky and Bullwinkle Movie*?"

"Love to," Minnie said, but she really didn't care. "What is it?"

Boris's eyes widened. "You never heard of Rocky and Bullwinkle?"

"It's a breakfast cereal, right?" Minnie guessed.

"No! Is classic American cartoon from early sixties!" Boris yelled. He was hurt she didn't know.

"Enough small talk," Fearless Leader said. "Look, Minnie Mogul. We're stuck in reruns. You're stuck without a project. Maybe we can help each other."

Minnie discretely touched the intercom on her desk. "Get me Security," she muttered.

"If you let us out of here," Boris said from inside the TV, "and we take over world, you make big movie and millions of dollars cash money!"

Minnie touched the intercom again. "Never mind," she said, canceling the security guards.

Fearless Leader shook the contract impatiently. "This gives you all rights to *The Rocky and Bullwinkle Show*. Now hurry up and sign so we can take over the world."

Minnie hesitated. "But I can't sign a contract that'll help three ruthless villains take over the world," she said.

"Why not?" they all said together.

"My pen's out of ink."

"Use mine," Fearless Leader said.

Minnie reached for the pen, and her hand went

through the glass TV screen like it wasn't even there. She grabbed the pen and signed the contract and then yanked her hand out. Lo and behold, along with her hand came the villainous trio.

Fearless Leader, Boris Badenov, and Natasha Fatale were out of the TV!

Even more miraculous, the cartoon TV stars had become real, live people!

"Hey!" Minnie exclaimed. She'd seen overpriced special effects before, but this was truly amazing. "How'd that happen?"

Fearless Leader, still clutching the contract, grinned through clenched teeth. "We're attached to the project."

From somewhere, an audience could be heard booing and hissing.

"Come on!" the real-person Boris complained. "Audience finds this unbelievable."

Suddenly they were pelted with eggs and tomatoes.

Minnie got up and steered the villains to the door. The contract she had signed was a done deal. But that didn't mean she wanted them hanging around their office. Minnie wished them well, Hollywood-style. "Keep in touch, babe," she said. "Love you. I mean that."

Satisfied, the villains headed for the front gate.

"Ah, the real world," Fearless Leader said, relishing his new incarnation as a human being. "Now for the next step in my plan to take over U.S.A."

Boris grinned widely. "Oh, I can't wait to take over U.S.A.!"

Fearless Leader gave him the evil eye.

"Oops, I mean help you take over U.S.A., Fearless Leader!" Boris said.

Natasha, batting her eyes said "U.S.A.? Fearless Leader, you will take over whole world! You will be king of planet!"

"King?!" Fearless Leader scoffed. "Who said I want to be king of the planet? Please. Call me 'premier' of the planet."

"Yes, Fearless Leader!" they chimed.

There was one small problem, however. Unbeknownst to the villains at the front gate, inside Phony Pictures, the studio boss P. G. Biggershot was reviewing Minnie Mogul's latest project, *The Rocky and Bullwinkle Movie.* "I don't like moose pictures," he said.

And that was that.

CHAPTER 3

Back in Frostbite Falls, in the cartoon house where Rocky and Bullwinkle lived, the not-so-famous Moose was jamming clothes into a suitcase.

"Where are you going?" Rocky asked him.

"I'm going to Washington to talk to the president about the trees!" Bullwinkle declared. He slammed the suitcase shut and marched out the door.

The road that ran by their house was backed up for miles. ROAD TO WASHINGTON said a sign. DELAYS AHEAD said another.

Red tape stretched across the road, holding the traffic at a standstill.

"Look at all the red tape!" Rocky cried.

Bullwinkle put on a brave face. "Don't worry, little buddy," he said. "I'm sure the president will send for us, after all the letters I wrote him. Why, I'll bet they're working on our case right now. Someone's bound to be here any minute now . . . or two . . . or three. . . ."

Bullwinkle was half right. Someone in Washington was working on their case. But it wasn't someone in the office of the president.

It was someone in the office of the FBI.

CHAPTER 4

It was a big office, with big windows, big plants, big chairs—and one very big problem. FBI Agent Karen Sympathy stood formally under the gaze of her steely-eyed boss. The nameplate on the man's desk identified him as Cappy Von Trappment. Below his name it read, HARD-BOILED FBI DIRECTOR.

Cappy wasn't happy.

"After all your failed assignments in the past," he said to the young woman, "I suppose you're wondering why I picked you for this mission."

Karen Sympathy had a reputation for being idealistic and warmhearted. She was kind. She was a good person. It was holding her back as an FBI agent. "Yes sir," Karen replied. She had no idea.

Cappy leaned forward, his expression grim. "This is your last chance," he said. "Your last chance to prove yourself, Agent Sympathy. This job will either make or break your career. It requires the model FBI agent: someone tough, someone hard-bitten, someone emotionless, someone"—his expression changed to curiosity—"What are you doing?!"

Karen smiled sweetly. "Watering your plants, sir? They seemed so thirsty—"

Cappy stamped his foot. "Never mind the plants! Let 'em die!"

"Yessir!" Karen said stiffly, dropping the watering can.

"Good," Cappy said. "I believe you're familiar with *The Rocky and Bullwinkle Show*?"

"Eeee!" Karen squealed. Cappy frowned. Quickly she changed her reply to, "Affirmative, I mean."

A few hours later Karen found herself at an important meeting at the White House. Seated in a darkened Oval Office, she watched attentively as Cappy began a presentation beside a big-screen TV. Watching with them were U. S. President Signoff, Federal Communications Commission Director Schoentell, Presidential Campaign Manager Eddie Measures, and three generals wearing four stars apiece on their military dress uniforms.

"Mr. President," Cappy explained, "you are watching a regular network TV station."

The screen showed the tail end of an election commercial. "President Signoff," the voice blared. "Standing firm in the middle of the road."

"But look what happens when we go to cable," Cappy said. He made the switch with the TV's remote. Now they were looking at a printed message on an otherwise blank screen: RBTV IS COMING! NOV. 7TH, ELECTION DAY! Cappy surfed the channels to show them that the same message, RBTV IS COMING, was on every cable channel. Then he switched the TV off and went to a slide projector.

"Mr. President, over the last six months a cartoon villain from the old *Rocky and Bullwinkle Show* named Fearless Leader has bought up every single hour of cable programming in this country." He showed two slides of Fearless Leader: one in his cartoon state, and one as he had become—a real human being.

"He's formed a giant network called RBTV, or 'Really Bad Television,'" Cappy went on.

"According to our sources," Eddie Measures told the president, "three days from now Fearless Leader plans to broadcast TV shows so terrible, they'll turn anyone who watches them into a mindless zombie incapable of independent thought."

"Totally different from regular TV," Shoentell rushed to clarify.

"If Fearless Leader can hypnotize viewers through their TV sets, he can go on the air and make the whole country vote him in as president," Eddie Measures warned.

President Signoff frowned. "Well, that's no good!"

"No sir," Shoentell agreed.

"I mean, I want to be president again," Signoff said.

"We know that, sir," Measures said.

The president turned to his generals. "Can't the Pentagon do something about this? Any recommendations? General Foods? General Store? General Consternation?"

The three generals just shrugged and shook their heads.

"What about the FBI?" Shoentell asked Cappy.

"'We've already sent three crack agents to infiltrate RBTV, and they've disappeared. It's almost as if they had a 'mole' in the White House," he reported, using the spy word for "enemy agent."

Next to the president a hairy mammal with a pointed snout and long fingernails for digging had appeared. It wore a plaid suit and took notes in a big pad. They had a mole, all right.

"That's ridiculous!" the president said.

"Yes sir," Cappy said respectfully. Mole or no mole, he wasn't about to argue with the president of the United States.

Relieved, the mole went back to his note-taking.

"What is it you recommend, Cappy?" the president said at last.

Cappy scanned the faces of the other men in the room, waiting to make sure he had everyone's attention. "The only chance we have is to send for the two gallant heroes who successfully foiled Fearless leader's schemes for world domination back when he posed a threat in the 1960s. If anyone can stop him, they can."

Karen squealed, "Rocky and Bullwinkle!"

The president and his men glared at her.

She cleared her throat and repeated the names with dignity. "Rocky and Bullwinkle."

"Mr. President," Cappy said, "this is Agent Karen Sympathy."

The president gave her a doubtful look. "Are you sure she can handle working with . . . Rocky and Bullwinkle?" He obviously held a very high opinion of the famous moose and squirrel.

"Don't worry, Mr. President. I assure you she's the right woman for the project. She's tough, she's committed, she's hard as nails, she's . . . put down the president's cat, Karen!"

Karen was holding the fuzzy little animal to her cheek, making kissy faces at it.

"Karen!" Cappy snapped, startling her, making

her drop the cat. It landed with a screech. "Good,"
Cappy said.

"Just checking it for wiretaps!" Karen fibbed to
the others.

They all seemed satisfied. For the time being, at
least.

CHAPTER 5

With the White House meeting behind them, Cappy and Karen were free to return to FBI headquarters, where the hard-boiled director gave his soft-spoken agent a final briefing.

"Your number one job is to get Rocky and Bullwinkle to New York," Cappy told her. "It's important to shut down this Fearless Leader character before his broadcast starts." Cappy checked his watch. "You have forty-six hours."

Karen nodded. "Thank you, sir. I won't fail."

"Be careful," Cappy told her. "We've already lost three of our best agents. Good luck, Karen."

"Oh, sir," Karen said. "Just one thing: How do I get Rocky and Bullwinkle out of reruns, into our world?"

Cappy seemed peeved. "I don't know! Fearless Leader and the other two got out, somehow, so figure it out! Remember: We only care about results."

* * *

Cappy's words rang in her ears as Karen's plane landed in L.A. a few hours later. From the airport she took a cab straight to the Phony Pictures studios in Hollywood. Minutes after her arrival at the gate she was in a meeting with Minnie Mogul.

"Sorry," Minnie told her, "I can't help you. The only way to get Rocky and Bullwinkle out of cartoon-world reruns is to get Mr. Biggershot to green-light *The Rocky and Bullwinkle Movie*. But he ain't exactly listening to me!"

Minnie lit a match and dropped it on a pile of scripts. It burst into flames.

Karen had come too far to give up that easily. She insisted on another meeting with Biggershot. This time it was two—Minnie and Karen—against one. "If you don't green-light *The Rocky and Bullwinkle Movie*," the earnest young agent told the overweight executive, "Fearless Leader will take over everything. The whole world is at stake!"

Minnie nodded.

Biggershot chomped on his cigar thoughtfully. Finally, he gave the verdict. "Who cares? The world stinks, anyway!"

That night, long after sundown, when the studio was dark and deserted, someone dressed in black,

25

cat burglar-type clothing emerged from the shadows alongside the high security fence that surrounded the Phony Pictures lot. With her she carried a black bag.

It was none other than Agent Sympathy.

"I'll green-light this picture myself if I have to," she muttered as she scaled the fence and rappelled down the side of a soundstage. Then she hurried across the lot toward a huge structure topped with big-lensed spotlights—the studio's lighthouse.

Moving quickly, she deftly dodged a pair of security guards, then opened her black bag and withdrew a tiny trampoline. She attached herself to it with a long cord and backed off to give herself a running start. She took off like a sprinter and then pounced, springing herself all the way up to a catwalk on the highest upper story of the lighthouse. Next she hoisted the tramp up and then picked a locked door to the lighthouse control room. In seconds the lock gave way, and Karen slipped inside.

She found herself in a large machine room dominated by an enormous green bulb. It was Phony Pictures's official green light, controlled from a panel of flashing switches and giant levers located just below it. A sign over the control panel warned,

STUDIO GREEN LIGHT! BIG SHOTS ONLY!
PLEASE ENTER NAME AND GENRE OF PRODUCT.

Karen went to it and scanned the controls—for the different Hollywood genre movies. She threw one labeled ROAD/COMEDY/FANTASY/ADVENTURE and typed the name ROCKY AND BULLWINKLE on the monitor.

She was actually green-lighting the movie.

The huge green light hummed. But before it could flare, the circuits were interrupted by alarms. Flashing lights—red and white—blinked wildly. Sirens screamed.

Down below, security guards gathered by the lighthouse. Karen grabbed the biggest lever of all and tried to pull it down. It was incredibly heavy. She gave it everything she had until it finally moved and the big green light flared and shone from the top of the lighthouse, casting a green glow over the entire studio.

Far away in cartoon land, Rocky and Bullwinkle stood by the side of the road outside their humble home.

They were still waiting patiently for a ride to Washington. Bullwinkle was still counting the seconds until the president would send his car. He was up to 15,724,824.

Rocky had had enough. "It's been six months!" he complained.

"Or 15,724,825 seconds," Bullwinkle said, "but who's counting!"

From far away came a faint rumbling sound. It sounded like rain on the way. Rocky sadly picked up his little suitcase and said, "Bullwinkle, I'm going home."

Bullwinkle put a hand on his friend's shoulder. "Okay, little pal," he said. "I guess you're right."

But as Bullwinkle and Rocky turned to leave, a strange thing happened. Down the crowded highway a ray of green light shone, cutting through the delay signs and frozen traffic. It swept Rocky and Bullwinkle off their feet and whisked them away like a tornado!

"What's happening?!" Rocky cried.

"The president must be beaming us to Washington!" Bullwinkle said happily in the green light.

"The president can't give the green light," Rocky said. "Only Hollywood can do that!"

Hollywood was fine with Bullwinkle. "And it only took thirty-five years from when we were canceled!"

KA-BLAM! The green light in the tower at Phony Pictures burst, and the building rocked with the blast. When the smoke cleared, Karen Sympathy was face-to-face with her heroes: Rocky and Bullwinkle!

"It's you!" Karen cried. "Rocky!" She picked up the waist-high squirrel and stared at him face-to-face. Then she put him down and went to the moose. "And Bull—" she started to say, trying to raise the six foot seven inch moose as she had the squirrel. "And Bull—" she said, trying again to lift him.

"I believe the word you're searching for is 'winkle,'" Bullwinkle said.

Karen's grin widened. They were here! She'd gotten them into the real world! For the time being she forgot all about the Phony Pictures security guards, who were racing up the steps.

"What network are you from?" Rocky asked Karen.

She flashed her badge. "Karen Sympathy, FBI."

"Oh, come now!" Bullwinkle scoffed. "Our show may have been corny, but I'd hardly call it a federal case."

"Listen guys," Karen said, glad to be the one to tell them that the world still needed their help. But there wasn't time. The clatter of the guards' boot heels on the staircase was getting too close. "They're coming!" Karen said. "We've got to get out of here, fast!"

Bullwinkle knew what to do. "Quick!" he said. "Let's cut to a commercial!" But nothing happened.

"What is this—PBS?" Bullwinkle said, still confused.

There was no time to explain. Security guards crashed into the room just as Karen, Rocky, and Bullwinkle escaped onto the catwalk. The FBI agent slammed the door behind them and withdrew an aerosol can labeled FOIL-A-GUARD from her bag. She sprayed its contents into the keyhole, where it hardened like cement, jamming the lock.

A guard trapped inside yelled angrily, "Hey! She gave *The Rocky and Bullwinkle Movie* a green light!"

Hearing that, Rocky and Bullwinkle turned face-to-face. "Movie?" they both said.

"Bullwinkle," Rocky said nervously, "I don't think we're on television anymore."

Karen lowered her long climbing rope from the railing. "That's right," she told them. "This is real life. Can you rappel?"

"Sure!" Bullwinkle said. "I've been repelling viewers for years!"

Karen rolled her eyes. "Come on. I'll help you down."

"What about Rocky?" Bullwinkle said.

"He's a flying squirrel," Karen reminded him. "He'll manage."

Bullwinkle and Karen held on to the rope and slipped down from the railing, heading for the long trip to the ground. When they finally landed and looked up, they saw Rocky still on the catwalk.

"Hurry up, Rocky!" Karen yelled. "Fly down!"

Rocky spread his arms and leaped off, yelling, "Just like old tiiiii . . ."

And he dropped like a stone.

SLAM! Rocky hit the ground.

"Oh, my God! Are you all right?!" Karen said. She and Bullwinkle helped the little squirrel to his feet.

"Sure," Rocky said, dazed. "Just . . . out of practice." Then the three of them rushed to the front gate, where Karen's convertible sports car was waiting.

CHAPTER 6

"I watched your show all the time when I was a little girl," Karen told our heroes as they drove off in her car.

She thought about the way she had looked then—small and thin—almost birdlike. A sweet little girl.

"It made me want to have adventures, and I guess that's why I joined the Bureau. Of course, that little girl doesn't exist anymore. There's no room for her kind in the FBI."

A voice inside Karen's head protested, "I do too exist! Let me out!" It was her own voice—as a child's voice—but she was a grown-up, so she ignored it.

"Where are we going?" Bullwinkle asked her.

"Our mission is in New York," Karen said. "We have to stop Fearless Leader's broadcast within forty hours."

Bullwinkle scratched between his antlers. New York was far away. "Why don't we take an airplane?" he said.

"Because then it wouldn't be a Road Movie," Karen told him. Plus she had a lot to talk to them about. "We don't know how," she began, "but Fearless Leader, Boris, and Natasha have escaped into the real world. We think he's going to hypnotize everyone and rig the presidential election. So the president sent me—"

"Of course!" Bullwinkle interrupted. "The president got my letters about the trees!"

"What trees?" Karen asked.

Bullwinkle showed her a photo of a cartoon stump forest. "The Frostbite Falls Forest. I knew he would respond!"

Karen frowned. "Look, we don't have time—"

Rocky tried to explain. "This lady isn't here about the trees, Bullwinkle. She's from the FBI."

"FBI? Didn't they take our show off the air?"

"You're thinking of the FCC. Federal Communications Commission."

"They didn't like it, either?" Bullwinkle said.

"That's not what I mean!" Rocky said.

"You mean they did like it?" Bullwinkle said.

"I don't think they ever watched it." Rocky said.

"And who could blame them?" Bullwinkle said

at last. He smiled at Karen. "Can you believe we used to get paid for joke routines like this?"

Karen was ready to blow up. "Would you listen to me, please?!" she yelled. Once again she tried to explain their mission.

Unfortunately, Bullwinkle was so focused on saving the forest, he simply couldn't understand. "You want us to hypnotize the president?" he said.

"No!" Karen gasped. Then she decided to do something completely out of character. She decided to tell Bullwinkle. . . . an untruth. A fib.

"Actually . . ." she said. "you're right! The trees . . . the president wants me because . . . he wants to head up the, er, Committee for the Animated Wilderness Preservation." It made her feel awful to lie.

"That's not what you said before," Rocky said, pouting. But before Karen had time to explain, they were interrupted by the sound of music playing somewhere. It was loud, with a jerky beat.

"What kind of music is that?!" Bullwinkle exclaimed.

"Hip-hop," Karen explained. She glanced at the car radio. "That's funny, it's not even on."

"Oh, that's just Bullwinkle," Rocky told her. "His antlers pick up everything. Cover your nose, Bullwinkle," he said.

Bullwinkle put his hand over his nose, and the music stopped.

"They don't have music like that in Frostbite Falls," Rocky told her.

Karen shook her head. "You haven't been out of Frostbite Falls for more than thirty years, have you? What's it like to be canceled?"

"It's like we fell asleep and woke up thirty years later, like Rip Van Winkle," Rocky said.

"You mean Rip Van Bullwinkle," said Bullwinkle.

"Have things changed very much, Agent Sympathy?" Rocky asked. He knew they had for Rip Van Winkle.

"Uh, a little," Karen said.

In fact, things had changed a lot since 1964. As day broke with a sound like plate glass shattering over the City of Angels, Rocky and Bullwinkle began to see that.

Music from one passing car shook the boys to their bones.

A family in a minivan passed, with everyone inside on cell phones.

And a billboard showing an immense purple dinosaur struck them with terror.

"Don't worry," Karen said. "That's Barney. He's a friendly dinosaur!"

No, the real threat wasn't Barney. It wasn't in Los

Angeles. The real threat was lurking somewhere on the other side of the country, in New York.

New York, where Fearless Leader was preparing for a staff meeting on the top floor of RBTV headquarters. They had taken over the old RCA Building, the birthplace of network television.

Natasha and Boris hurried down the hallway. "Boris, dollink," she cooed, "you are natural-born TV executive."

Boris's face broke into a wide grin. "I told you all those years of bad taste and dirty double-crossing would pay off!" he said.

Together the villains went into the control room, where Fearless Leader stood before a complicated-looking machine. Several studio technicians were on hand, as well as a couple of Hollywood producers and several Pottsylvanian spies.

"This," Fearless Leader told everyone, "is Quality Control. It will enhance or degrade the quality of whatever you run through it."

Boris and Natasha shared a greedy look. This was going to be fun!

"If the input show is bad enough," Fearless Leader continued, "Quality Control should exaggerate its mind-numbing properties until the audience is completely hypnotized." Then he turned his evil eye toward Boris. "So, Badenov, these shows had better be terrible."

"Don't worry, Fearless Leader!" Boris said. "We hired professional television producers." If anybody could make a bad show, it was them.

The producers responded to the comment with a schmoozy "thumbs-up." They knew they could do it.

"Plus, we brought writers and actors over special from Pottsylvania," Natasha added. "All former spies like us."

The spies in the room waved.

Fearless Leader seemed satisfied. "We're ready to test the machine, then," he told them. "Everyone, put on our protective glasses!"

Everyone in the room put on a pair of huge sunglasses.

Boris adjusted his and smiled. "Natasha—you know what is difference between you and me?"

"What's that, Boris?" she said.

Boris waggled slyly. "I make this look bad," he boasted.

On an overhead TV screen the RBTV company logo appeared. An announcer with a heavy Slavic accent said, "Coming to your TV on November seventh! Three exciting shows of the highest fun!"

Then a daytime talk show appeared. In it, a spy host chatted with three spy guests before a live spy audience. Everyone wore black trench coats.

"To enjoy watching others suffer in the daytime,

there is *The Jenny Spy Show*," the announcer said.

The sound went up on the talk-show host, a dark, glamorous woman. "So, Tatiana, did you know your husband, Igor, was double agent?"

Igor was seated next to Tatania. He handed her a bouquet of flowers. She accepted it, then slammed him over the head with it.

Fearless Leader smiled. It was only the first show, and it was stupefying.

"Next time," the announcer interrupted, changing the channel, "if adventure is your best ingredient, try the action with the show *Clever Spies Crush the Enemy,* on Monday.

The TV showed a zoom lens close-up of a sports car ramming a wall and exploding. The Quality Control machine hummed with sinister energy.

Fearless Leader was delighted. The second show was just as mind-numbing.

"And last of all," the announcer said, switching channels again, "the laughing never gets away with the show *Three Funny Wacky Spies & Their Horse, Who Will Also Be a Spy.* The screen showed three men in black hats and trench coats standing beside a horse, also wearing a black hat and trench coat.

The third show was dumb enough to send a rock into a coma.

The Quality Control machine glowed. The audience in the screen room was totally hypnotized, brain-dead, and motionless, with glazed-over eyes. A few even had drool hanging from their mouths. RBTV was working perfectly. According to a scale on the machine, the audience had gone from Bored, to Apathetic, to Hypnotized, all the way to Total Zombification.

"It works!" a technician cheered, and everyone clapped. Fearless Leader threw his head back and laughed. Then, suddenly, his PC began to beep.

"Silence!" Fearless Leader commanded. "It's a message from my mole at the White House!"

The printer attached to his personal computer spat out a sheet of paper. On letterhead that said OFFICIAL WHITE HOUSE MOLE was a message from their spy. Fearless Leader read it and handed it off to Boris and Natasha, who read it too. The news was not good.

Together they cried, "Moose and Squirrel!"

Fearless Leader's eyes misted over as he focused on that distant horizon that only would-be tyrants can see. "Moose and Squirrel," he said. "How many times in the past have they stood between me and my dreams of glory? How many times have they foiled my plans with their bungling interference?"

Boris raised his hand like a schoolboy and answered, "Twelve times?"

Fearless Leader gnashed his teeth. "Quiet,

39

idiot!" he yelled. "They must never reach New York City alive. I want you to destroy them personally!"

Boris was flattered. "After thirty years of waiting, one more chance to crush Moose and Squirrel!"

Natasha looked relieved. "Oh, Fearless Leader," she said, "you're so good to us!" And she and Boris followed him out the door.

"There has never been a way to actually destroy a cartoon character," Fearless Leader confided in the spies as they walked down the hallway, "until now."

"What about in movie *Roger Rabbit*?" Boris pointed out.

"Shut up!" Fearless Leader snapped. "This is totally different!" Then he repeated exactly as before, "There has never been a way to actually destroy a cartoon character, until now!"

Before them a ten-year-old girl wearing thick glasses appeared. In her hands was a sinister-looking machine.

"This is the Computer Degenerating Imagery," Fearless Leader told Boris and Natasha. "Show them, Sydney."

The girl nodded confidently. "Computer Degenerating Imagery—or CDI as we call it—is totally user-friendly. Simply index the binary codes of the animated image you wish to degenerate and the CDI will create pulse specially encoded to dismantle the digital image of your film stock."

Boris and Natasha stared stupidly.

Sydney rolled her eyes. "Read the book," she said, slapping down a thick instruction manual. "I assume you're both computer literate?"

They remained silent.

CHAPTER 7

Outside the RBTV building, the infamous Boris Badenov and his equally infamous assistant, Natasha Fatale, roughly tossed the CDI and its huge instruction manual into the back of a van.

"We don't need computer weapon to kill Moose and Squirrel!" Boris said. "We've already been trying to kill Moose and Squirrel for thirty-five years."

"Of course, dollink!" Natasha agreed, slamming the passenger side door behind herself. "We're experts!"

Away they drove down the Avenue of the Americas. Boris imagined the image of Fearless Leader's face reflected in the glass windows of the office buildings along the way.

At that very moment the real Fearless Leader sat alone in an immense studio back at RBTV headquarters. He flipped a switch on his desk, activating two robot cameras.

"Dear Diary," the evil commander said. "Soon the presidency will be mine. With Moose and Squirrel out of the way, there will be nothing to stop me. As for this FBI Agent Karen Sympathy, I will deal with her the way I dealt with the three agents before her. At the moment of truth, she will be plugged directly in the Quality Control current and turned into a helpless, mindless vegetable. . . ."

For now, at least, Karen was safely far away in Monument Valley, driving with her heroes.

"Y'know, I used to be just like you guys," Karen told the moose and squirrel as they traveled along. "Cheerful, optimistic . . . but if there's one thing the Bureau taught me, it's that life is not a cartoon."

Just then, an enormous safe fell from the sky and crashed into the road, barely missing them. Karen jerked the wheel and swerved around it, then came onto a dozen lit bundles of dynamite in the road. More packages came hurtling down from the cliffs above them.

Boris and Natasha were bombing them from above. As the bundles of TNT began to explode, the villains hurried into their van.

"Out of the car!" Karen cried.

"What's the rush?!" Bullwinkle wanted to know.

Karen flung the car door open and shoved the moose and squirrel out, then hopped out her side and rolled as the car sailed over the cliff and blew up in the gully below. "Are you guys all right?" she asked, dusting herself off.

Rocky and Bullwinkle shrugged. "Of course we're all right. We're cartoons." they said.

"Guess I should have figured as much," Karen muttered.

"But not for long!" came a gravelly voice behind them. Karen, Rocky, and Bullwinkle turned and found themselves face-to-face with Boris and Natasha.

"Hey, Rock," Bullwinkle said, "they look kinda familiar."

"Yeah," Rocky said. "Haven't we seen those two somewhere before?"

It had been almost forty years.

Karen walked up to the darkly dressed duo and examined a cannon they just happened to have with them. Putting a hand on her hip, she asked coyly, "What's with the cannon?"

Boris and Natasha answered together, at once, "Is traditional." Then Boris touched a match to the cannon's fuse, and Natasha put her fingers in her ears.

"Run!" Rocky and Bullwinkle cried.

Karen stayed put, however. "Boris Badenov," she said, flirting, "I've seen you on TV. You're a crooked, creepy, crummy—"

"Oh, thank you," Boris said.

"Slimy, sneaky, sleazy—"

"Stop!" Boris giggled. "You flatter me!" He failed to notice as Karen secretly wet her fingers and touched the cannon's fuse, fizzling it out.

"You're a sadistic spy and a rotten person!" Karen said finally.

Boris was overcome with ecstatic giggling. "No more!" he begged. "You embarrass me!" Then he put his fingers in his ears to shield them from the blast he was expecting from the cannon.

Karen, Rocky, and Bullwinkle took the opportunity to hop into Boris and Natasha's van.

A second later, Boris and Natasha removed their fingers from their ears. "Where is boom?" Boris wondered aloud.

"All I hear is truck starting," Natasha said. She and Boris watched their vehicle pull away and head down the highway. From the open door in back, primitive weapons—mallets, frying pans, a crossbow—fell by the side of the road. Natasha picked the CDI out of the litter. "Boris, dollink," she said, "maybe is time to update our technique."

Just then their portable video phone rang. Boris switched it on, and Fearless leader appeared on the screen.

"Fearless Leader, how's tricks?" Boris said, as if all were well.

"This is not a call for chitchat, Badenov!" Fearless Leader growled. "Did you liquidate Moose and Squirrel?"

"We tried to use new machine," Boris lied, "but the digital . . . thingy . . . was out of electro-synch with . . . scuzzy . . . floppy bus."

"Are you talking to me?" Fearless Leader said, threatening, gangster-like. "Are you talking to me? There's no one else here, so you must be talking to me . . . and you're lying! Catch Moose and Squirrel and next time use the CDI on them! That's the only way you can destroy a cartoon! And, Badenov, you remember what happened to the last Pottsylvanian spy who lied to me?"

"Comrade Goofinov?" Natasha said.

"Former Comrade Goofinov," Fearless Leader corrected.

"Ho, boy," Boris said with a sigh.

CHAPTER 8

Meanwhile, on the desert highway, Karen and the boys continued their journey east in Boris and Natasha's van.

"We can't ride to the rescue in a stolen truck," Rocky complained.

"Yeah, Karen!" Bullwinkle agreed. "Why couldn't you steal something with bucket seats?"

"Bullwinkle!" Rocky scolded.

"Just kidding, Rock," the moose said.

"It's just not right," Rocky said.

"Not right?!" Karen said. "What are you talking about?! They wrecked our car! They were trying to kill us!"

That didn't matter to Rocky. "We're supposed to be the heroes," he said.

"It's not 1964 anymore," Karen told him. "You're in the real world now. Besides, hard-boiled FBI agents don't steal, they 'commandeer.'"

Bullwinkle was on Rocky's side. "Two rights don't make a wrong, Karen," he said.

Rocky held his head. "That's not what you mean," he said.

"You mean two rights do make a wrong?" Bullwinkle asked.

"Bullwinkle!"

"I always thought two rights made a U-turn."

Karen had just about had enough. "I don't know how much more of this I can take," she said.

Bullwinkle knew what she meant. "Imagine how the people reading this book must feel," he said.

"Look!" Karen said. "All I want from you guys are results, okay?!" She was trying hard to be hard-boiled, like her boss.

"Okay," Bullwinkle said. "Your hair is too long."

Karen looked puzzled.

"And those shoes don't match your handbag," he went on.

"No, Bullwinkle," Rocky said. "She said RE-sults. Not IN-sults!"

"I thought it was a strange request," Bullwinkle said.

"Do you really think my hair is too long?" Karen said, worried.

And so across the U.S.A. they went. Over the

Great Divide in the Rockies. Into Colorado. Onto the Great Plains and into Oklahoma. There, they came upon a highway rest stop with a McDonald's, a Burger King, a Hardee's, and several other fast-food franchise restaurants.

Rocky and Bullwinkle had never seen anything like it. In their time, rest stops were quiet places with public rest rooms, not fast food-emporiums.

"What a strange-looking town," Rocky said.

Meanwhile, several states behind them, Boris and Natasha tramped along the road.

"If only we had a helicopter," Boris wished aloud, and sure enough, they spotted a helicopter down the road, parked on a landing pad outside a row of portable toilets.

"Natasha, quick!" Boris cried. They dashed for the chopper, its keys conveniently left in the ignition. The pilot burst from one of the portable toilets just as the villains Boris and Natasha lifted off.

"Great googly moogly! Who the heck—" the pilot said.

Quickly the helicopter raced away, giving the villains a bird's-eye view of the surrounding countryside. From this altitude, finding our heroes was as easy as spotting a bug on a road map.

"There they are, on Interstate One. Just outside

of Red Bait, Oklahoma," Natasha said to Boris, who was doing the driving. "Using helicopter was brilliant—you are such cheater, dollink!"

"I love it when you call me 'cheater,'" Boris said.

"State police?" Natasha said into a radio set on the chopper. They had spotted the van below. "This is FBI Agent Karen Sympathy," she lied. "My FBI I.D. was just stolen by beautiful lady with curly blond hair, riding in stolen truck with cartoon moose and flying squirrel who can't fly."

The voice of a state police dispatcher responded immediately. "Thanks, Agent Sympathy. We'll get on it right away. Over and out."

Boris and Natasha snickered with evil glee.

In the van below, Karen was apologizing. "I'm sorry I yelled at you guys," she was saying. "But you don't understand. I can't mess up this time."

"This time?" Rocky said. "Was there a last time?"

Karen blushed. "Let's just say I've made . . . mistakes. The last terrorist I apprehended wanted to call his mother to tell her the bad news. So I loaned him my calling card."

"What happened?" Bullwinkle asked.

"I never saw him again," Karen replied. "Except two weeks later I got a phone bill with forty thousand rubles in charges. I can't blow this one—the whole world depends on it. And I can't do it without your help."

Rocky gave her an encouraging smile. "You can count on Bullwinkle and me," he said.

That made Karen feel better. "Good," she said. "You know, I'm glad Cappy sent me to find you guys. I think we're gonna make a great team."

Just then, a police siren blared.

Karen pulled the car over, and the cop car came up behind her. Out jumped two policemen and a cameraman.

"Oh no," Karen said. They were from a "true crime" cop show on TV. One that showed video-tapes of real arrests.

"Get out of the car with your hands up!" one of the officers said. The cameraman was getting the whole arrest on film.

""It's okay, officer, I'm with the FBI!" Karen yelled, showing her badge.

"Out of the car, now!" another cop said.

The cameraman continued to make his jumpy, video film as the first cop, a burly plug of a man, pulled Karen out and handcuffed her. Rocky and Bullwinkle stood by, their faces automatically blurred by the camera to protect their identities.

"Hey, Rock," Bullwinkle commented, "your face is all blurry."

"So's yours," Rocky said.

The cops were focusing their attention on the driver. "This truck matches the description of a vehicle stolen outside Red Bait, Oklahoma, just a couple of hours ago," the big cop told Karen.

"You're under arrest for grand theft auto and for impersonating FBI Agent Karen Sympathy."

Karen's eyes blazed. "But I am FBI Agent Karen Sympathy!" she yelled.

"Don't give us that," the cop said back. "The real Karen Sympathy has a heavy Pottsylvanian accent. We heard it on the radio."

Rocky couldn't believe what was happening. "She really is with the FBI," he insisted.

"Yeah, right, and I'm the famous television actor John Goodman," the cop said, dragging her into the police cruiser.

"I thought you looked sort of familiar," Karen said as he slammed the door behind her. She was definitely going to jail.

"But we're a team!" Rocky protested. "Wherever she goes, we go!"

"Don't worry, Karen," Bullwinkle whispered. "We'll appear at your trial as character witnesses. Animated character witnesses!"

"No," Karen told them bravely. "It's your duty to get to New York by eight P.M. tomorrow."

"We can't leave you, Karen," Rocky said.

"Hey, I'm an FBI agent," she reminded him. "I'll straighten this out and catch up with you later."

"But we've never been in the real world before!" Rocky said, worried.

"You'll do great," Karen told him. "I know it."

The cops slammed the door on her and jumped in the squad car.

"You can't just leave them on the side of the road!" she said as they drove off. "They don't even know where they are."

The big cop scoffed. "They're animals. They'll forage."

But Rocky and Bullwinkle weren't ordinary animals—they were cartoon animals. In the real world they could be pretty helpless. The buzzards were already circling overhead.

But Bullwinkle wasn't ready to give up. "Come on, Rock," he said. "Time's a-wastin'. We owe it to Karen to see the president about the trees!"

"Trees? Bullwinkle, we have to go to New York," Rocky argued. "We don't have time for Washington!"

"Rocky, this is no time to worry about getting the washing done," Bullwinkle said.

"Not washing DONE. Washing-TON."

"Ton?! That's a lotta laundry. Can't we just take it to the dry cleaners?"

"What dry cleaners? I'm talking about Washington, D.C."

"So am I. D. C. Dry Cleaners."

Rocky rolled his eyes. "Bullwinkle, that joke won't wash."

"Well, you can't blame me for drying," Bullwinkle answered with a twinkle in his eye.

"I think I'll fly ahead," Rocky said, straining. But the out-of-shape squirrel never got off the runway. The situation looked hopeless.

"I've got a plan!" Bullwinkle said suddenly.

"What is it?" Rocky asked.

"Help!" Bullwinkle cried. "Helllp! Somebody! Hellllllp!"

It was a daring plan, and it would have worked if not for the fact that they were five hundred miles from the middle of nowhere. No one could hear them. So on they walked, two lone figures making their way through a foreign and hostile live-action landscape.

They walked until their feet ached. They hitch-hiked until their thumbs ached. They stood in the middle of the road until a Greyhound bus ran over them, and everything ached. Then, out of the darkness, came a ray of hope.

Actually, it was headlights.

Two college students named Martin and Lewis pulled to a stop and let the boys into the back seat.

"So, where do you boys go to school?"

Bullwinkle asked, struggling to get his tall body under his seatbelt

"We're undergrads at Wossamotta U.," Martin replied.

Rocky and Bullwinkle were stunned. "Wossamotta U.!"

"I went there!" Bullwinkle said.

"He was a big football star," Rocky told the boys.

Lewis looked back. "I thought you seemed familiar."

"Where are you coming from?" Rocky asked.

"We've been on the road," Martin told him. "Looking for America."

"Yeah, we've been looking all weekend," Lewis added.

"We can't find it," Martin said.

"We're exhausted," Lewis said.

Bullwinkle didn't understand. "Gee, fellas, maybe America is all around you in a thousand different beautiful manifestations."

As he said it, they sped past bright neon-light signs for fast-food restaurants: McDonald's, Burger King, Hardee's.

Martin and Lewis laughed. "Yeah, right!"

Bullwinkle stared at the fast-food signs zipping by. "Hey, Rocky," he said, "haven't we passed this town before?"

CHAPTER 9

High above our heroes a helicopter passed, transporting the villainous Boris and Natasha over the Illinois landscape to the campus of Wossamotta U. There it landed, on the football field. Boris got out and ran to where a wobbly old man—the college president—awaited.

"For you," Boris said, handing the old man a check—a donation to the college made in the name of Bullwinkle J. Moose! Then Boris and Natasha followed him across the campus to his office.

"I always liked that Bullwinkle," the old man cackled, signing the moose's name onto a diploma. He planned to bestow him with an honorary degree at an upcoming ceremony at the college.

Boris was counting on it. That's why he had made the donation in Bullwinkle's name in the first place. "When Moose is at podium for acceptance speech, I'll be up in water tower with CDI," Boris told Natasha after they had left the president's office.

Unfortunately, Wossamotta U. did not have a water tower. Boris couldn't even find a water fountain. There was only one thing they could do: They immediately donned work clothes and set about constructing a water tower across the graduation area.

Meanwhile, back in the town of Red Bait, Oklahoma, Karen had been convicted and sentenced to five years at the women's prison farm for grand theft auto and impersonating a federal agent. She tried calling the home office in Washington, but all she got was Cappy's voice mail.

"Sir, it's Karen Sympathy," she recorded into the machine. "I'm in jail in Oklahoma and I only get one phone call a week, so—"

That's where the machine cut her off, saying "Mailbox full. Please try again later."

Karen stared at the telephone. Her situation seemed hopeless. "I love the new millennium," she said. November 7, the day Fearless Leader was scheduled to begin taking over the world, was only a day away, and she was stuck in prison. There was one consolation, she discovered, while digging in the prison potato field: One of the guards, Ole, was incredibly handsome.

"What's a nice girl like you doing in a place like this?" he asked her.

"Oh, five to ten," Karen replied, flirting. "Twenty, if I'm lucky."

Meanwhile, on the road to the college, Martin and Lewis's Sebring sports car was getting a fax.

"Heavens to Betsy!" Bullwinkle cried as the sheet of paper curled out. "The car is sticking its tongue out at me!"

"It's just a fax," Martin said.

"A what?" Rocky said.

Lewis raised an eyebrow. "Don't you guys know about faxes?"

"Yeah, and E-mail?" Martin said.

"Sure," Bullwinkle said. "A fax is a little red critter that steals geese and chickens. Half of them are males, and other ones are E-mails."

Lewis chuckled. "No. They're a way of transmitting computer-generated information across great distances in the blink of an eye."

"Well, I was close," Bullwinkle said.

Martin handed the fax back. It was for Bullwinkle.

"Holy smoke!" Rocky cried, reading it.

"Wossamotta U. wants to give you an honorary degree.

"And the ceremony is today!" Bullwinkle shouted gleefully.

"We don't have time to go," Rocky told him. "We've gotta get to New York."

"It's only a short detour from here," Bullwinkle said.

"I guess if it's in the name of education," Rocky said, and that was that.

A short while later they were strolling the grounds with the president.

"Everything looks the same, but different," Bullwinkle said.

The president knew what Bullwinkle meant. "Wossamotta U. has been a live-action campus since 1964," the old man said. "Been that way ever since the show went into reruns. And I'm afraid there's still a lot of anti-cartoon feeling on campus these days. . . ."

They turned a corner and saw an unruly crowd of students gathered. TV crews were at hand. Student with megaphones were perched in trees.

"Holy smoke!" Rocky exclaimed. "It's some kind of demonstration. What are the kids protesting these days?"

"Is it a civil rights march?" Bullwinkle guessed.

"An antiwar rally?" Rocky guessed.

It might have been either one, had this been the early 1960s. But, in fact, this was an anti-moose march. A raging controversy had broken out among the students that very morning over the decision to give Bullwinkle an honorary degree. It had brought out every watchdog and special interest group—the local left; the local right; and members of the local Anti-Animation League, who were afraid Bullwinkle's presence would turn the clock back thirty-five years. "Two, four, six, eight!" they chanted. "We don't wanna animate!"

"How dare they call him 'Moose'!" a student yelled through a megaphone.

"No more moose quotas!" yelled another.

"Gee," Bullwinkle said, showing them his book, *Bullwinkle's Familiar Quotations.* "I was just gonna look up a few more quotas for my speech."

"Gee, Bullwinkle, I guess it's true," Rocky said sadly. "You can't go home again."

Suddenly they were noticed. A student yelled, "Look! There's the animated freak now!" and the crowd roared angrily.

"My fans!" Bullwinkle declared happily.

"Those aren't fans," Rocky told him. "That's an angry mob!"

"So are my fans," Bullwinkle said simply, and he headed for the rostrum. In the face of danger, the antlered hero bravely made his way to the front.

A short distance away, Boris and Natasha were putting the finishing touches on the water tower.

"But is not a real water tower," Natasha said. "Why do we have to fill it with water?"

"I'm a stickler for authenticity," Boris snapped.

CHAPTER 10

Hundreds of miles away, Agent Karen Sympathy was trapped behind bars at the rough, tough women's prison farm outside Red Bait, Oklahoma.

It could have been a bad experience. It could have been an outrageously miserable experience.

But Agent Sympathy lucked out.

Somehow, someway, Karen had caught the eye of Ole, the simpleminded but incredibly handsome prison guard. He had looked into Karen's eyes and fallen madly in love with her.

At first Karen thought it might be her imagination. Ole was so cute and sweet. What could he see in an FBI-agent-turned-criminal like her?

But what had happened in the lunchroom made her think

Instead of the usual prison food that everyone else got, Karen was served poached salmon, scalloped potatoes, and fresh garden salad with homemade dressing.

That had to be Ole.

The girl in Karen was tickled pink.

The FBI agent in her began to plot her escape.

Her big chance came right after lunch. She was assigned KP duty, washing dishes in the prison kitchen.

Ole was assigned to watch her.

Karen washed, and Ole dried, and for a while they didn't speak; they just smiled shyly at each other.

At last Karen got up her nerve.

She promised Ole she would let him take her to the movies . . . if Ole would help her break out of jail.

Ole shyly brushed soapsuds off Karen's nose. Her offer was tempting, but helping a prisoner escape was a big deal. It was a lot to think about. "If I helped you, and you did escape, could we hold hands in the movie theater?" he asked hopefully.

"Of course we could, Ole," Karen said with a warm smile.

Ole smiled, too, then frowned. "But . . . how could we eat our popcorn?"

Karen tried not to roll her eyes. "We could eat popcorn with one hand and hold hands with the other," she explained patiently.

Ole smiled, then frowned again. "But . . . what if I want a soda?"

"Look," Karen said, trying not to lose her temper, "I'm sure we can work this out."

A short while later, Ole drove a hay truck to the prison gate. Hidden deep in the hay, Karen trembled and crossed her fingers. Would the guard let them through? Or would he discover her hiding in the back of the truck?

Ole waved at the prison guard. He smiled back and waved Ole through.

Yes! Karen thought as they drove through the prison gates. Ole was so sweet and innocent and honest, the guard probably never dreamed that the big Swede would be capable of helping a prisoner to escape.

Karen felt a stab of guilt. She'd led Ole astray.

But the FBI agent in her brushed the thought aside. National security was at stake. Bad guys from an old cartoon show were about to take over the world!

Could she reach Rocky and Bullwinkle in time to save the day?

CHAPTER 11

If Karen Sympathy was going to help Bullwinkle, she would have to hurry. At Wossamotta U., the ceremony had begun.

The college president surveyed the throng of angry students. Soon he would be handing out diplomas. Bullwinkle was seated right behind him on a folding chair.

Little did any of them know that Boris Badenov was climbing a nearby water tower at that moment, with evil on his mind.

"Good morning, students," the college president began. "Today Wossamotta U. honors one of our own—"

"Le boooo!" Some students from the front row threw baguettes at Bullwinkle.

Yes, even the French exchange students were angry.

"We 'ate you, Bullwinkle!" they cried.

Other students threw more mundane fare at Bullwinkle: eggs, tomatoes, an occasional taco with all the fixings.

The college president didn't pay any attention.

But Rocky kept his eyes open. Sitting on the stage behind his friend, the flying squirrel anxiously studied the crowd of students.

He was looking for signs of the kind of danger that usually appears halfway into the running time of this particular type of adventure.

Suddenly Rocky spotted a terrifying image: a short, fat guy dressed all in black near the top of the nearby water tower. "Hey!" Rocky gasped aloud. "That guy's not a college student!"

No one else seemed to notice. The college president continued his speech. "And so we are proud to present this honorary degree to Bullwinkle J. Moose."

No one could see it through the moose's thick brown fur, but Bullwinkle was blushing as he stepped up to the podium. He opened his mouth to speak . . .

And out came the voice of Frank Sinatra singing the song "Strangers in the Night . . ."

The students looked around. They were mystified.

Bullwinkle wasn't. His antlers were picking up

music from nearby radio stations again!

Bullwinkle covered his nose, and the music stopped.

"Good morning, children," Bullwinkle addressed the college students.

"Boooooo!" Calling college students "children" was a good way to start a riot! "BOOOOO!"

Suddenly Rocky jumped to his feet. "Bullwinkle, look out! It's a trap!"

But Rocky's high-pitched voice couldn't carry over the shouts and boos of the student body, especially when combined with the *splats* and *bonks* of flying fruit and vegetables.

And at the very moment that Bullwinkle rested his white-gloved cartoon hands on the podium, Boris Badenov reached the top of the water tower.

Boris's evil laugh scattered the birds perched along the water tower's room. He was prepared to destroy his nemesis once and for all.

CHAPTER 12

Boris clutched the high-tech CDI in one pudgy little hand.

He held the CDI instruction manual with the other.

His smile slipped a bit. Modern technology in the real world was fantastic. But it was so complicated!

In cartoon world, he thought, all we do is push big button and everything goes *BOOM!* In real world, I gotta know what the heck I'm doing!

He checked the contents page, then quickly turned to page seven.

"Hmm, 'Getting Started . . .'" he read out loud. "'Power switch A is located left of com port two. See diagram three-A.'"

Huh? Boris let out a breath. "Ho, boy. Maybe I shouldna slept through Spy Gizmo class back at Pottsylvania Community College!"

Down below, Bullwinkle rambled on . . . and on . . . and on about saving the cartoon forest. There was only one thing to do.

Rocky pulled his blue leather flying goggles down over his eyes. He was going to try one more time to summon those faded aeronautic skills that once made him a household name.

In other words, he was going to try to fly.

Rocky jumped down from his seat on the stage. He clenched his fists. (He could do that because, unlike real squirrels, cartoon squirrels have fingers.) Beads of sweat sprang from his forehead as he strained dormant muscles.

I can fly! he told himself. I can fly!

Rocky's tiny gray body began to vibrate.

He pushed himself as never before. . . .

But was it too little, too late?

For just then—high above the stage—Boris Badenov managed to turn on the CDI. "Aha!" the evil fiend cried. "Do I know computers or what?"

Boris aimed the CDI on the biggest target in sight: a six-foot-tall commencement speaker with antlers the width of an exit door.

With his grubby fingers on the computer's mouse, Boris laughed. "With this mouse, I kill Moose."

Could this be the end of Bullwinkle?

CHAPTER 13

But, wait—!

Boris hadn't counted on the get-up-and-go of Rocky the Flying Squirrel. Especially when his best friend was in trouble!

"Got to—save—Bullwinkle!" Rocky gasped.

Wobbling like a poorly thrown Frisbee, Rocky swooped into the air over the heads of the crowd.

Flying is just like riding a bike, Rocky tried to tell himself. Once you learn, you never really forget, right? . . . right?

Not exactly.

Rocky spread his arms wide, trying to steer.

But his aim was way off, and he headed straight toward the gathered students.

The students screamed and ducked as Rocky accidentally buzzed them like a crop-dusting airplane.

Just enough time to let Boris click his mouse.

There was only one problem.

Boris double-clicked. Strange words appeared on the computer screen:

BAD COMMAND OR FILE NAME.
PRESS ANY KEY TO CONTINUE.

Boris frowned. He frantically jabbed at the keyboard. "Which one is the 'Any' key?" he said.

That gave the trembling Rocky the extra moments he needed.

Was it skill, luck, or pure accident?

Rocky never knew. But he zoomed past Boris and bumped the CDI. With a single blow, he sent the computer hurtling through the sky.

Boris yelped. He reached for it, stepping off the water tower . . . and forgot one very important thing.

He looked at the empty space below him. "I ain't a cartoon no more."

He dropped like a rock.

He landed with a crash on top of the French exchange students.

Seconds later . . .

Clunk!

The CDI fell on his head.

Natasha rushed to his side.

About this time, Rocky was careening down,

also. I can land, I can land, I can land . . . , he told himself.

But he couldn't stop—he couldn't remember how to put on the brakes. "Mayday!" Rocky warned. Seconds later . . .

Rocky crash-landed on the stage, knocking over several octogenarian professors in the process.

The crowd cheered.

Oblivious to the crash landing behind him, Bullwinkle thought the applause was for him. "You like me!" he gushed. "You really like me!"

But even though the gallant squirrel had saved the day, he was having a moment of doubt.

He picked up his fallen goggles. "Maybe I should hang these up for good. I think I've lost the knack."

Bullwinkle resumed his speech. "Yes, without trees, where would the birdies live? Forced to migrate to the cities, they might take jobs away from local pigeons. And we all know what that would lead to . . . 'birdgeoning' unemployment . . ."

The crowd listened intently.

"Bullwinkle!" Rocky exclaimed, totally surprised. "They're listening!"

Yes, Bullwinkle's speech was so ridiculous that the students could not understand one word he was saying, and therefore found nothing to object to.

Cheering students rushed the stage. They lifted

Rocky and Bullwinkle to their shoulders and paraded them around campus.

But while the students cheered our heroes, Boris Badenov lay in the Wossamotta U. student infirmary, hovering on the brink of death.

Two beautiful nurses fussed over Boris. They put Band-Aids on his head. Natasha frowned nearby.

"Fix the boo-boo," Boris cooed to the nurses.

Natasha was mad, now. The nurses were flirting with Boris. She was thinking about giving them a few boo-boos of their own.

And so, after a memorable day at their alma mater, Rocky and Bullwinkle said a fond farewell to the ivy-covered walls of Wossamotta U.

"Don't forget to write, old buddy," Bullwinkle said.

"Bullwinkle," Rocky said. "Who are you talking to?"

Bullwinkle patted the ivy-covered wall. "I don't know, but it's like talking to a brick wall."

The college president shook Bullwinkle's hand. "I want to thank you boys for bringing unity back to this troubled campus with your ludicrous remarks."

Bullwinkle beamed.

Rocky scratched his head, trying to decide if that was a compliment or an insult.

Martin and Lewis made their way to the front of the crowd.

"Rocky, Bullwinkle," Martin said, "Lewis and I would like to say—"

"That before we met you guys, we had totally lost faith in America," Lewis said.

"Plus, we lost faith in our future—" Martin said.

"Yeah," said Lewis. "Plus, we lost faith in some of these girls we've been going out with."

"Yeah," said Martin, "and then I lost faith in my car—"

"Right?" Lewis said.

"Right?" Martin said. "Like, I used to think our car was really cool, but then, like, I just totally lost faith in it."

"But since we met you guys—" said Lewis.

"Yeah," said Martin.

"We love our car again," Lewis said.

"Yeah, man, like, the car is back," said Martin.

"And we would like, as a gesture, for you to have it," said Lewis.

"Yeah, so take the car," said Martin. "It's yours."

Rocky took the keys. "Well—gee, fellas, thanks!" said Rocky.

Rocky and Bullwinkle piled into the sleek convertible. Bullwinkle took the wheel.

"Er—but, you know how to drive, right?" Lewis said.

"Please," Bullwinkle said. "What moose can't drive an automobile?" He turned on the ignition and stepped on the gas . . .

Wham! He drove the car straight into the building. Bullwinkle flew over the windshield into the ivy-covered wall.

Rocky was embedded in a passenger-side air bag.

"Never said I was a good driver," Bullwinkle muttered through the ivy.

Bullwinkle peeled himself off the wall as only a cartoon character can do.

Yes, he had certainly left an impression on his old alma mater. An impression of a six-foot moose with antlers in the ivy on the walls.

With a final wave, Bullwinkle got back into the car, backed up—*SCREECH!* and took off—*SCREECH!* toward New York City.

As a cloud of dust and exhaust filled the air, Natasha was just helping Boris Badenov limp out of the student infirmary.

"Stop!" Boris yelled, forgetting all about his limp. He and Natasha ran top speed toward the chopper.

Meanwhile, back in Cow Tip, Oklahoma . . .

A hay truck pulled up outside the town's only movie theater. But not just any hay truck. A hay truck driven by a prison guard who could barely keep his eyes on the road for mooning over the pretty escaped convict at his side.

Agent Karen Sympathy glanced at her watch. Time was running out. She's have to pull a fast one on the slow but handsome prison guard. "Ole," she said sweetly, slipping her arm through his, "why don't you get the tickets, and I'll go park the truck?"

"Gosh, Karen," Ole gushed. "I've never had so much fun in my whole life. It's like—it's like there was always a little boy trapped somewhere inside me, and now that I've met you, I can finally let him out. It's like after years and years of looking, I finally met a girl that I can trust."

Karen smiled weakly as she looked into Ole's eyes.

Sighing happily, Ole at last was able to tear himself away from Karen long enough to get out to buy their tickets.

Karen slid behind the wheel. The little girl in her was really throwing a fit. How can you trick sweet, innocent, trusting Ole this way? Karen was overwhelmed with guilt.

But she was an agent of the Federal Bureau of Investigation. She had a job to do. An important one.

There was no time to go all ga-ga over a tall . . . handsome . . . sweet . . . country boy. She stole one last peek at her cute, adorable prison guard.

Ole looked back at her and waved.

Karen gulped and waved back.

As Ole turned back to the ticket booth to pay for their tickets, Karen took a deep breath, sent the protesting little girl inside of her to time-out, then put her foot down on the gas and drove away, past every empty parking spot, straight out of town.

Without looking back.

Back at the ticket booth, Ole turned around with his tickets clutched in his hand. He was ready to start his first real date with the girl of his dreams, his one true love, his . . .

Ole blinked and looked around.

Where was she?

Ole shifted to the other foot, still clutching the tickets.

He'd waited a lifetime for a girl like her. He didn't mind waiting a few more minutes.

CHAPTER 14

Meanwhile, our heroes, Rocky and Bullwinkle were gently motoring along an Illinois highway.

All over the highway, actually. Bullwinkle was not the best driver, and Rocky was eternally grateful for that new invention—seat belts.

A few minutes later they passed a huge rest stop made up of dozens of fast-food restaurants.

"Hey, Rock," Bullwinkle said, confused. "There's that same town again!"

Rocky rolled his eyes. "It's not the same town. Every town in America looks the same nowadays." Rocky sighed. "What happened to Mom and Pop?"

Bullwinkle looked back over his shoulder as the restaurants disappeared in the distance. "They must have retired and moved to Florida!" However, Bullwinkle was still driving. The car swerved all over the highway. They nearly ran a BMW off the road.

"Bullwinkle!" Rocky cried. "Look out!"

"Crazy driver!" shouted the man driving the BMW.

Bullwinkle jerked the steering wheel hard to the right toward an exit sign that said CHICAGO.

"Bullwinkle," Rocky said, "we're not going to Chicago!"

"We are now!" Bullwinkle replied.

The car plowed through the exit sign and flew onto the ramp, heading for the Chicago skyline.

Rocky buried his face in his hands.

But a side trip to Chicago was the least of his worries.

Little did our heroes know that Boris and Natasha's helicopter was beating the skies directly overhead.

Back at the Red Bait Prison Farm, Agent Karen Sympathy's daring escape had not gone unnoticed.

The warden decided she needed help finding her way back. He sent out a huge squadron of police cars that peeled out onto the highway, their sirens wailing.

Not too far away, at the Cow Tip Movie Theater, Ole was still standing in the same spot on the sidewalk, clutching his two tickets.

The movie was over. All the other folks had gone

home. Ole had watched the constellations pass overhead, and the sun come up. Now people bustled around him, heading to school or work or running morning errands.

But Ole was a patient man. He kept on waiting.

He knew how hard it could be sometimes to parallel park a big truck.

He knew Karen would hurry back to him. Yep, any minute now . . .

Karen was hurrying. But not toward Ole. She was driving the old hay truck in the opposite direction, down the interstate highway that cut through Indiana.

Soon she passed a sign that read, DE BITTER, IND. She had to slow down as she drove through town.

A crowd had gathered on the sidewalk. What could be so interesting in a tiny town like this? she wondered.

Funny, they were all standing stock-still. Almost like they were . . . hypnotized!

Karen slammed on the brakes. No. It couldn't be! She backed up and stared in disbelief.

The entire crowd—men, women, and children, even dogs and cats—stared in the store window at a huge television.

They were watching *The Jenny Spy Show.*

No one moved. Or laughed. Or even blinked.

It was happening already. America was being hypnotized by their televisions.

There was no time to lose.

Karen jammed on the gas pedal and zoomed out of town.

CHAPTER 15

"You are watching the premier broadcast of RBTV!" an announcer proclaimed as the RBTV logo—a spinning world—twirled on the screen.

In the New York studio of RBTV, Fearless Leader's lackeys were watching the same broadcast as the folks in DeBitter, Ind. But not one of them became hypnotized.

In fact, they burst into applause.

Their secret? Simple. They were wearing the special protective sunglasses that blocked the hypnotic rays from RBTV programming, rendering them harmless.

Fearless Leader—wearing his own pair of very cool protective shades—did something most people had never seen him do: He smiled. A teeny, tiny smile. "Ah," he breathed, "I love my RBTV."

The logo faded, and *The Jenny Spy Show* came back on.

"Fearless Leader!" came a voice from the doorway to his office. It was one of the spies working in the Commercial Time Sales Department. "Reports show that thirty percent of the country are already total zombies!"

"Good!" Fearless Leader leaned back in his chair. "I'll address the nation at eight P.M., eastern time." He checked his watch. "Seven central and mountain." He thought. "Six Pacific time. Five Guam. Three Vladivostok. Noon Pago Pago. Five A.M. Uzbekistan. Two-thirty Husker Du . . ."

Where were our heroes?

They'd just burst onto the bustling boulevards of Chicago, Illinois. Cars swerved. Pedestrians leaped out of the way. Bullwinkle drove like a Pottsylvanian cabdriver.

WHOMP-WHOMP-WHOMP-WHOMP. The sound of a helicopter echoed in the canyons between the skyscrapers.

Boris and Natasha were there.

Natasha flew the chopper while Boris read the CDI manual.

Suddenly Natasha spotted something on the ground. "There they are!"

Boris frantically read the manual. He was still trying to figure out his computer problem so he could use the high-tech equipment to destroy his enemies. He kept getting the message: BAD COMMAND OR FILE NAME.

He flipped to page sixty-three and found the heading "Troubleshooting. Bad Command or File Name."

Aha! This would tell him what was wrong and how to fix it. With new hope, he read aloud, "'You have typed in a bad command or file name. Type in the correct command or file name.'"

Boris turned red and hot. He slammed the manual closed. Forget modern high-tech technology. I'll take care of Moose and Squirrel old-fashioned Pottsylvania way, he thought. "Natasha," he shouted. "I have new plan. Smush them!"

Natasha's heart fluttered. Boris was so handsome when he was being dastardly!

"Duck!" Rocky cried when he saw the chopper dropping out of the sky. Natasha caught up with them from behind and swept over the car, snagging the windshield with her landing gear and lifting it right off the dashboard.

Rocky and Bullwinkle popped up into a strong wind.

Again Natasha steered the helicopter in low, this time ramming the car onto a sidewalk, where people scrambled to get out of the way.

"Bullwinkle, look out!" Rocky cried. They were coming to a wall, and beyond that, the Chicago River.

First, however, they had to run over a couple of fruit carts—and the identical twins who owned and operated them.

"LOOK OUT!" the Cliche brothers screamed, diving away.

ZANG! The Sebring made a ramp of their carts and sailed over the wall and into the water beyond.

CRUNCH! The car crash-landed on the other side of the Chicago River.

"WHEW!" Bullwinkle said. Fortunately, he and Rocky had bailed out halfway across. It would have been a perfect escape—except for . . .

S-S-S-SUCK! The sewage pipes that sucked them under.

Ten blocks away they burst out of a hydrant and caught each other in midair.

"I think I'm getting the hang of this driving thing, Rock," Bullwinkle said as they end-over-ended. The flatbed truck with the Sebring onboard appeared below them, and they dived for it. They hit the seats just as Natasha's helicopter appeared overhead.

Boris leaned out with the CDI, and then . . . his hand stilled on the mouse. The black-hearted villain had paused to savor the moment.

The no-good spy had spent a cartoon lifetime chasing those two do-gooders. Now, at last, victory was at hand. With one double click of the CDI computer's mouse, he would destroy his enemies forever.

Boris cackled with devilish delight.

Click-click!

Suddenly—like magic—the buildings all disappeared.

The city of Chicago no longer existed.

The helicopter hovered like a hummingbird in a blank blue space.

Natasha squealed.

Boris's evil-minded brain reeled as it struggled to understand. "Hey! What happened?"

Suddenly two giant bearded heads poked through the infinite blue nothingness. Like giant dinosaurs, they peered through the glass windshield of the helicopter.

"What are you doin'?" one big head exclaimed in exasperation.

The other big head rolled his eyes.

"Who are you?" Boris and Natasha gasped.

"I'm the Digital Effects Coordinator at Industrial Light and Magic," said Big Head #1. "We're adding the backgrounds with a computer. Who took out the buildings?"

"We've been working on your helicopter chase

scene for three months!" Big Head #2 complained.

Boris and Natasha exchanged glances. These guys were computer artists. They seemed to be saying that their whole chase was just special effects.

"Boris," Natasha hissed. "You degenerated wrong special effect."

Boris blushed. "Whoops."

"Whoops?" Big Head #1 shrieked. "Do you know what this is costing us?" Just then his eyes widened as he seemed to notice the helicopter for the first time. "A helicopter?! We can't afford that! That's not in the script!"

Natasha shrugged. "We improvised," she explained.

Big Head #1 turned off the helicopter blades. Boris and Natasha hung in midair.

"Okay, click on Undo to restore the buildings," Big Head #2 instructed Boris. "And don't worry—we'll take care of the helicopter."

"That's a little more like it!" Natasha said.

The giant faces of the technicians pulled back, disappearing into the blue sky.

Still frozen in the air, Boris clicked on the CDI mouse.

In an instant they found themselves back in the bustling city of Chicago, exactly as before, but with one small difference . . .

Boris and Natasha looked at each other. They

were suspended in midair. Fifty feet above the street.

And the technician had kept his word.

"No helicopter!" they both said at once.

With a yelp, the cartoon characters-turned-humans dropped toward the street like stones.

Yes, it could have been curtains for both of them if not for a traveling mattress salesman who just happened to be passing by below with three deluxe mattresses strapped to his back. "Mattresses!" the hunched-over salesman called out. "Get your mattresses!"

A man ran over, fumbling for change. "How much?"

FOOMF! FOOMF!

Boris and Natasha landed on the top mattress, flattening the salesman beneath them.

The customer stared in disbelief.

And Rocky and Bullwinkle headed out of the city . . . while Boris and Natasha were forced to rent a car to resume the chase.

Luckily for our heroes, the penny-pinching spies chose the Cheapo Rent-A-Car Agency. The stack of paperwork they had to fill out to rent the car was thicker than the CDI instruction manual.

Rocky and Bullwinkle got a head start on their way to a reunion with Karen. It happened at an intersection crowded with fast-food restaurants—McDonald's, Burger King, Hardee's, and a Pizza Hut.

The flatbed truck carrying Rocky and Bullwinkle in their car approached from the north.

And Karen's hay truck approached from the west.

WHAM! They collided in the center. It was a beautiful reunion.

"And in our favorite town," Bullwinkle said.

On the flatbed, Bullwinkle put his car in reverse. As the truck rumbled across the intersection, Bullwinkle's car flew off the back. It landed right in the middle of an intersection—

Right in front of an oncoming truck.

An oncoming hay truck driven by FBI Agent Karen Sympathy!

Karen slammed on the breaks and screeched to a halt, just barely avoiding a horrible crash. She jumped out of the truck and stormed over to give the driver a piece of her mind. "Hey, why don't you look where you're"—then her eyes popped open wide—"Rocky! Bullwinkle!"

"Karen!" Rocky and Bullwinkle cried.

Karen was so surprised, she threw her arms around them and gave them both a huge hug. "Guys, I missed you so much!" she exclaimed. "I was so worried about—"

Stop! something inside her ordered.

Karen froze. FBI agents didn't act like this! She had to control herself if she ever wanted to make a success of herself in the agency.

Clearing her throat, Karen stepped back, straightened her jacket, and stuck out her hand for a formal handshake. "I mean, good work, Agents Rocky and Bullwinkle." Then she told them the bad news. "We have six hours to get to New York. RBTV is already turning people into zombies."

Rocky glanced at Bullwinkle. The moose didn't seem to find it strange that they had run into Karen in the middle of an intersection in the middle of nowhere in the middle of Illinois.

But Rocky did. He hesitated to bring it up, but . . . he had to know. "Karen . . . why aren't you in jail?"

A blush began to creep up Karen's neck, but her FBI training allowed her to stop it cold before it reached her cheeks. Then she did what all good FBI agents do when they find themselves in a tight spot: She fibbed. "I . . . was pardoned."

The instant the words tumbled from her lips, a dozen police cars roared up and squealed to a stop, surrounding them from every direction. Cops, reporters, and cameramen swarmed out.

One cop raised a bullhorn to his mouth. "Put your hands up—now!"

Bullwinkle scratched his head. "This is a pardon?"

Karen winced.

Meanwhile, the country was plunging deeper and deeper into Fearless Leader's sinister grasp. . . .

In typical middle-American homes, typical American families were spending a typical evening watching TV together. Except their eyes were glazed over—even more than usual—as they tuned in to *Clever Spies Crush the Enemy* on Monday.

People in sports bars and pizza parlors drooled in their drinks, their eyes glued to what Fearless Leader wanted them to see.

The hypnotic programming had even reached the French exchange students, Martin and Lewis and the college president at Wossamotta U. as they sat in front of the big-screen TV in the student lounge.

Was no one safe from Fearless Leader's mad scheme to take over the nation?

Could no one stop him?

Only three people, maybe. Or, rather, one person, one moose, and one squirrel.

But our heroes were caught up in a jam as sticky as molasses: a small country court of law.

The hot, crowded courtroom was packed with reporters, photographers, and townspeople simply curious about all the fuss.

Our heroes sat at a long, wooden conference table in front of the judge.

Karen just sat there, stunned. "My gosh, what am I doing in the FBI?" she said. She fought back tears as she turned to Rocky and Bullwinkle. "Look at me, I'm a failure. I got you both into this mess. I don't have what it takes to be an agent."

"Cheer up, Karen," Rocky said cheerfully. "We believe in you. Without you, we wouldn't be here today—"

"Facing thirty years to life in the tank," Bullwinkle pointed out.

Karen groaned and laid her forehead on the table.

Just then the room hushed as an elderly man with thick glasses and a hearing aid entered the room. As he sat down at the front of the room, Rocky read the nameplate on his desk: JUDGE CAMEO. He hoped the old man would be kind.

The bailiff stood at the front of the room. "The states of California, Arizona, New Mexico, Colorado, Kansas, Oklahoma, Missouri, Illinois, Indiana, and Ohio, versus Karen Sympathy, Rocket J. Squirrel, and Bullwinkle J. Moose. Judge Cameo presiding."

The judge banged his gavel. "Who speaks for the defense?"

Bullwinkle stepped forward. "Bullwinkle J. Moose for the defense, Your Honor." Suddenly, in a way that only makes sense in cartoons, Bullwinkle was wearing a long black robe and a white wig, the traditional uniform of a lawyer from long ago.

The courtroom tittered at his silly appearance.

Karen and Rocky exchanged an uneasy glance. This was a tricky case. Could Bullwinkle handle it?

Judge Cameo banged his gavel again. "Come to order! The defendants are charged with"—he picked up a long list and adjusted his reading glasses—"grand theft auto. Breaking out of jail. Speeding—two counts. Compromising the character of a prison guard—two counts. Criminally bad puns—eighteen counts. Not sticking to the script—three counts. Talking to the audience—nine counts. And one count of making a mockery of a major motion picture."

"I object!" Bullwinkle cried, jumping to his feet.

The judge frowned.

Bullwinkle smiled politely. "Shouldn't that be three counts?"

Rocky rolled his eyes, and Karen buried her face in her hands as the courtroom erupted into laughter.

Judge Cameo banged his gavel again. "Counselor! Call your first witness."

"Yes, Your Honor." Bullwinkle turned dramatically. "As our first witness, the defense calls"—his eyes scanned the courtroom—"Karen Sympathy!"

"Oh, please no," Karen whispered.

But Rocky patted her hand, and Karen made her way to the witness stand. She raised her right hand.

The clerk repeated the oath required of all witnesses: "Do you, Karen Sympathy, swear to tell the truth, the whole truth, and nothing but the truth, so help you God?"

Karen nodded. "I do."

"Hah!" Bullwinkle shouted dramatically. "A little late!"

Karen's jaw dropped.

Laughter filled the courtroom.

Rocky slapped his forehead. Whose side was Bullwinkle on, anyway? He tried to catch his friend's eye, but the moose was on a roll.

Bullwinkle strode forward. "Ms. Sympathy, isn't it true that when our convertible was destroyed in Monument Valley, the first thing you did was steal somebody else's truck?"

Karen glanced nervously at the judge. "Um, that depends on how you legally define the word 'steal.'"

"And," Bullwinkle went on, "didn't you escape from prison by telling that poor, trusting prison guard that you would let him take you to the movies?"

Karen squirmed in her seat. "Well . . . I thought we might have time. . . ."

Bullwinkle paced the front of the courtroom, his black robes flying. "And didn't you tell me and Rocky that you got out of prison because you got a pardon?"

"Yes—yes—I did do that!" Karen fought not to break down.

"And isn't it true," Bullwinkle shouted, just inches from her face, "that you have no respect for the law or for anything else?"

"No!" Karen cried. "I was just trying to complete my mission! I was only supposed to care about results!"

Karen was nearly broken as Bullwinkle rose to his full height. "And one final question!" he boomed.

Everyone in the courtroom was on the edge of his seat.

Karen braced herself.

"How come Rocky and me are still cartoons and Boris and Natasha aren't?"

"I don't know!" Karen cried, nearly sobbing, broken at last. "I didn't make up this story! I'm only one of the characters!"

Bullwinkle turned on his heel to face the district attorney. "Your witness, counselor," he said dramatically.

The D.A. was totally confused. He was supposed to argue against Ms. Sympathy. But this six-foot moose—who was supposed to defend her—had instead used up all his arguments to convict. "Er—the plaintiff rests!" the confused D.A. said, and quickly sat down.

Bullwinkle strode to his seat and sat down next to his friends.

Rocky was so flabbergasted, he could barely speak. "Bullwinkle, you're supposed to be the defense attorney. You just proved we're guilty!"

"Yes, but now our consciences are clean," he said. "And the healing can begin."

"Your Honor," said the D.A., "it's time the court showed the world that no special treatment will be given to celebrity defendants. Let us—"

"Celebrities?" Judge Cameo exclaimed. "Did you say the defendants are celebrities?" He yanked off his glasses. "By cracky, I must have on my reading glasses." He searched his desk, then switched to another pair. After adjusting his hearing aid, he squinted at Rocky and Bullwinkle. "Stars above! It's Rocky and Bullwinkle!" Judge Cameo exclaimed. "Why, I used to love your show!"

Bullwinkle beamed proudly.

The judge reached for a huge black book on the corner of his desk. He blew the dust off it, then flipped through the pages till he found what he was looking for. "Mr. District Attorney, may I remind you of the penal code, paragraph twenty-three, section C." He cleared his throat and read: "'Celebrities are above the law.'" He slammed the book. "Case dismissed!" He banged his gavel, and the courtroom erupted into chaos.

Karen and Rocky cheered and threw their arms around each other. They couldn't believe it. They were free!

Bullwinkle was disappointed. "That's it? But I didn't get to use my insanity defense!"

But, fortunately, that was it, and moments later our heroes were back on the road, basking in the sunshine of freedom, with three hours left to get from Rapid Froth, Ohio, to New York City.

"Three hours?" Karen gripped the steering wheel of Rocky and Bullwinkle's car and groaned. "If only we had an airplane."

If only . . .

Rocky, Bullwinkle, and Karen sighed.

Suddenly Rocky sat up in his seat and pointed straight ahead. "Look!"

Miraculously, a mere twenty yards ahead, was a sign that read,

AIRPLANES FOR SALE—
CHEAP!
ASK FOR "JEB"

"Gee," Karen said. "Another lucky break."

Following the directions, Karen soon pulled the car to a stop outside an old ramshackle trailer. Behind it, a beat-up little one-propeller plane sat sideways in a dusty field.

Karen shaded her eyes against the slanting rays of the late-afternoon sun as she got out of the car and looked around. That's when she spotted a very old man dressed in dusty, tattered overalls sitting in an old rocking chair on the porch of the trailer. He looked about a hundred, and he looked as if he hadn't moved in weeks.

He's gotta be Jeb, Karen thought.

"Afternoon, folks," Jeb said, barely moving.

"Hi," Karen said in a friendly voice. "Got any planes left?"

Jeb turned very, very slowly. Karen could swear she could hear his old bones creak. He gazed for a moment at the single plane sitting in the overgrown field. "Well . . ." he drawled, "let's see now . . ."

Karen tried to be polite. This was a lucky break,

after all. But their time was running out.

Then something caught her eye. Karen shaded her eyes and glanced at the horizon.

In the distance a huge dust cloud billowed above the highway. Somebody else was coming down the road.

Ice-cold goose bumps prickled along her spine, but she waited patiently for old Jeb to do business his way.

The car sped closer. Probably a tourist, Karen thought. They'll pass us by without a thought. . . .

Jeb put his hands on the arms of his rocking chair, as if to stand up.

By then the car was close enough for Karen to spot two familiar faces through the windshield.

Karen gasped. It was Boris and Natasha, in a cheap rental car—and it was traveling straight for them!

There was no time to lose, no time for slow, country-style manners. Karen shoved some money into Jeb's bony hands and hustled Rocky and Bullwinkle across the weed-choked field toward the plane. "Keep the change!" she called over her shoulder. To her friends, she ordered, "Let's go!"

Jeb stared at the money in his hand, then actually got up out of his rocking chair to holler after them, "Hey! You can't all get in there! She won't hold the weight!"

But, unfortunately for our heroes, Karen couldn't hear the old man's warning. She had already started the noisy motor and was taxiing the plane across the field.

The Cheapo Rent-A-Car roared past Jeb, trying to cut her off, trying to keep the plane from taking off into the air.

"We've got them, Boris!" Natasha shouted gleefully. "We've got them!"

"They've got us, Rocky," Bullwinkle shouted woefully. "They've got us!"

But just as Boris and Natasha were about to catch up with the tiny plane . . .

The rental agreement on their car suddenly expired.

Instantly their cheap rental car was surrounded by the dedicated agents of the Cheapo Rent-A-Car Agency. Cheapo agents dressed in cheap beige jackets jumped out of their Cheapo cars, waving clipboards at the two stunned spies.

The Cheapo agents insisted that the driver do one of two things: Return the rental car immediately, or immediately renew the rental agreement.

What could they do? They had to renew. Fuming, Boris and Natasha feverishly tried to fill out the huge stack of renewal forms as they watched our heroes' plane pick up speed.

With a clunky roar, Karen's plane began to lift off.

Boris and Natasha, rental agreements in hand, ran after it.

But it was too late.

The plane—and our heroes—took off into the blue sky.

"That was a close one," Rocky said, glancing down.

"Let's just hope this thing makes it all the way to New York," Karen said with a worried frown. She'd never flown a plane before. Crossing her fingers, she steered the plane toward the Big Apple.

Back at Jeb's place, Boris and Natasha—depressed, dejected, and downhearted—sat down on the runway.

"Where did we go wrong, Boris?" Natasha moaned. "We tried to blow them up . . ."

"We tried to have them arrested . . ." Boris added, nodding miserably.

"We tried to degenerate them . . ."

"We tried to smush them . . ."

"And we never even came close." Natasha shook her long black hair back from her face and sighed. "Boris, dollink, what are we doing? We been trying to catch Moose and Squirrel ever since we first got drawn. We tried to stab them, shoot them, smash them, smush them, crush them, bash them, mash them, and squash them." Her bottom lip trembled. "And they don't even know our names!"

Blinking back tears, Natasha grabbed Boris by the lapels of his little black suit. "I'm tired of all this, Boris! I don't want to be spy no more. Let's face it, dollink—we stink! We can never catch Moose and Squirrel."

Boris was stunned by Natasha's outburst.

"Oh, Boris, don't you want to have a little Boris? A little Natasha? Wouldn't it be wonderful?" She wrapped her arms around his neck and pressed her pale cheek against his. "We'll rent a cottage by the Sea of Pottsylvania and teach them how to lie and cheat and be rotten. They will be worst children in the world! They will be little monsters. It will be awful!" She sighed, smiling in delight at the fantasy. "Oh, Boris, we could be so happy!" She sat back and stared expectantly into his beady black eyes.

Boris was speechless! He opened his mouth—

RING!

His spy phone!

"Hoo-boy," Boris muttered. "Saved by bell!" He quickly turned on his phone, glad for the interruption . . .

. . . until he saw who was calling. Fearless Leader's terrifying face smiled back at them from the phone's small square video monitor.

Boris cringed.

His boss was sitting in his RBTV studio in New York, getting made up for his television broadcast. Behind him, the studio swarmed with activity.

"Well, Badenov? Did the CDI work?"

Boris rubbed his sore behind, remembering his fall from the sky. "Oh, it works all right!" he muttered.

"Good!" Fearless Leader replied. "So—Moose and Squirrel are dead, then?"

Boris choked. He stared helplessly into Natasha's eyes, trying to fabricate some quick explanation.

But it was no use. He had to face facts. He was a big, fat Pottsylvanian failure! "Oh, Fearless Leader, we tried everything, but—"

"Yes, Fearless Leader!" Natasha interrupted, shoving her face in front of the screen. "We killed Moose and Squirrel!"

Boris's eyes nearly popped out of his head.

Natasha put a fingertip to her lips.

Boris had no idea what she was up to. But he quietly obeyed.

"Excellent," Fearless Leader crowed. "Wait

there for my private jet. I want you both by my side for the big broadcast." And with that, Fearless Leader signed off.

Boris gasped, totally confused. He had never understood female Pottsylvanian spies. But now he understood Natasha even less. "Why did you tell him—"

Natasha's eyes shone brightly. "Boris, don't you see?" she exclaimed. "Moose and Squirrel can't possibly reach New York by eight P.M. And suppose they did? How can they stop us? We've won, Boris! We've won!"

Boris frowned in confusion, then . . . he chuckled in devious delight. "Of course!" he said. "Just like I planned it!"

CHAPTER 16

Meanwhile, our heroes' little plane put-put-puttered through the darkening sky. The motor began to sputter. The plan dipped and jerked as it flew.

Karen fought with the controls, trying to keep the plane steady. "She won't pull up!" she exclaimed. "We're too heavy!" What could they do? "Rocky," she said, "can you fly Bullwinkle down?"

Rocky looked at her in disbelief. "Karen, he's a moose!"

"I beg your pardon," Bullwinkle said. "I'm as trim as a young fawn."

Rocky shook his head. "Bullwinkle—you weigh four hundred pounds!"

"Four hundred imaginary pounds," Bullwinkle pointed out.

Suddenly a horrible grinding noise growled deep from the plane's gut. The cockpit's controls spun wildly.

Karen, Rocky, and Bullwinkle felt a terrifying drop. Then the plane began to lose altitude.

"Bullwinkle," Karen exclaimed, "can you fly an airplane?"

"Please," Bullwinkle said. "What moose can't fly an airplane?"

Karen turned to the flying squirrel. "Rocky, you'll have to fly me down."

Rocky panicked. "I—I can't do that, Karen. I can't fly anymore! I've lost the touch!"

But Karen knew there was no other choice. The plane was barely clearing the treetops now. If the plane didn't lose some of its weight, they'd all go down. "Bullwinkle," she said firmly, "take the controls."

Bullwinkle got up into a crouch to move into the pilot's seat.

"Listen to me, Rocky," Karen told the flying squirrel as she switched seats. "You can do this. All you have to do is believe in—aaaggghhh!"

Unfortunately, despite being imaginary, Bullwinkle's four hundred-pound weight pitched the plane to one side.

Karen lost her balance—and was thrown out of the cockpit.

Rocky couldn't bear to looked down. But he forced himself to.

Thank heavens! Miraculously, Karen had managed to grab hold of the wing. She dangled from the tip.

Suddenly a huge billboard loomed ahead of them. It had a huge picture of the president and the words FOUR MORE YEARS OF SIGNOFF.

"Look out for the sign!" Karen screamed.

The plane's cloth wing ripped.

This time, Karen plummeted toward the ground.

CHAPTER 17

"Karen!" Rocky shrieked.

There was no time to think. The hero in Rocky responded to a person in need.

Rocky pulled his goggles down over his eyes and crawled toward the plane's door. "Here goes nothing!" And with one brave swoop, he dived out of the plane.

Down below, Karen saw the ground rushing up at her. It looked like certain death. . . .

She shut her eyes tight. She didn't want to look!

And then . . . she felt something stop her fall.

She opened her eyes. It was Rocky! He had caught her in his arms.

Struggling with her weight, Rocky flew Karen over the billboard, just barely clearing it.

Bullwinkle wasn't so lucky.

SLAM! Bullwinkle crashed the plane into the bill-board, smashing through President Signoff's picture and out through the other side.

"Bullwinkle!" Karen and Rocky cried.

The big moose stuck his head out the window. "Never said I could fly it well! See you in New York!"

Dusk was falling as Rocky and Karen soared over the outskirts of New York City. Karen's feet dangled within inches of houses, chimneys, and telephone poles.

"Can't you fly any higher?" she asked anxiously.

"I'm trying!" Rocky said. He hoisted her up and carried her aloft in his arms.

Rocky grinned. He was starting to feel the wind in his leather helmet straps again!

"Rocky!" Karen said. "You're flying! You're flying!"

"I am?" Rocky looked around. "I am! Look at me! I got the old juice back!"

He turned on the speed and soared high into the sky. Rocky flew with a joy he hadn't known for years.

The lights of the city winked on as he and Karen soared past the Statue of Liberty.

They flew up Wall Street with skyscrapers looming around them. They flew past parks and apartment buildings, delis and theaters.

The city seemed quiet and peaceful. . . .

WAIT A MINUTE!

Karen and Rocky did a double take. New York City? Quiet and peaceful?!

By the time they reached Rockefeller Center, Karen and Rocky could tell something was wrong. Terribly wrong.

The whole city of New York was completely zombified.

At Rockefeller Center's famous ice-skating rink, all the skaters were staring, hypnotized, at a giant TV showing RBTV.

"Rocky," Karen warned, "whatever you do, don't look at the screen!"

Rocky flew her gently to the ground, careful not to look at the huge TV.

Karen checked her watch, then searched the sky above her. "Oh, Rocky, where's Bullwinkle? Fearless Leader's speech starts in five minutes."

"I knew we shouldn't have left him," Rocky said anxiously. "Bullwinkle and I have never been apart in thirty-five years!"

Karen bit her lip. The little girl in her wanted to hug him and tell him not to worry, everything was going to be all right.

But you can't be an FBI agent and act like that, she scolded herself. So, instead, she said in a tough voice, "Hang in there, Squirrel. Right now America needs you!"

Rocky stared up at the RBTV building. "But how are we gonna find Fearless Leader?"

Karen rubbed her chin. "Gee, if only there was just one more coincidence. . . ."

Rocky rubbed his chin, too. If only . . .

Suddenly—

SCREECH!

Right before their eyes, a shiny red stretch limo pulled up to the entrance to the building. A chauffeur hopped out and quickly ran around to the other side to open the door to the backseat.

Boris and Natasha stepped out.

"Come, Natasha," Boris said, taking her arm. "Follow me to Fearless Leader."

But first they put on their protective sunglasses. Then they strutted like movie stars into the building.

Rocky let out a low whistle. "Gee, this chin-rubbing stuff really works!"

Now all they had to do was tail Boris and Natasha into the building. Surely the spies would lead them to Fearless Leader.

But what would they do when they got there?

Karen didn't have a clue. But somehow she and one small flying squirrel would have to find a way to stop the ruthless Fearless Leader and his army of spies from taking over the entire country.

CHAPTER 18

Upstairs, the RBTV studio was a flurry of activity. Dozens of Pottsylvanian spies—wearing protective sunglasses—prepared for the upcoming television broadcast.

Fearless Leader sat at his desk, surrounded by hair and makeup artists. He was in a very good mood. Success was only minutes away.

Ah, television. What was it, after all? Just a silly little harmless box. A box you could plug in to the wall—and plug in to the world.

In the right hands, it could educate. Entertain. Inform. It could bring people all over the world closer together through shared experiences. It could take people to a sold-out soccer match, to a congressional debate, to the depths of the ocean, to the moon . . .

But in the wrong hands . . .

Fearless Leader held up his own two gloved

hands, sneered, and chuckled ruthlessly.

Television could destroy the mind. And bring a nation to its knees.

And, to Fearless Leader, that was a very entertaining idea, indeed.

He glanced at the clock on the wall. Tonight's prime-time special—starring Fearless Leader in his private little chat with the American people—was about to begin.

CRASH!

Just then, Boris and Natasha burst into the room.

"Fearless Leader, we're ba-ack!" Boris said with a big smile. "You are soooo happy to see us!"

"Fearless Leader," Natasha cooed, "when you take over U.S.A., I want to be secretary of state. And Boris wants to be surgeon general."

"If you ask me," Boris said smugly, "congratulations are in order! We took care of Moose and Squirrel. Is no way they'll ever stop broadcast!"

CRASH!

Everyone froze as the door burst open again.

Boris gulped. "Uh-oh . . ."

FBI Agent Karen Sympathy and Rocket J. Squirrel—the squirrel Boris had just bragged about annihilating—ran into the room.

Karen flashed her badge. "FBI! Anyone who's a Pottsylvanian spy, put your hands up now!"

Everyone in the room threw up his hands.

Everyone . . . except Fearless Leader. He kept his hands hidden in his lap, gripping the remote control. "Congratulations, Badenov," Fearless Leader said sarcastically.

Natasha blushed. How humiliating!

Boris trembled in his boots. What would Fearless Leader do to them? The possibilities were too horrible to imagine!

But Fearless Leader had more important issues to deal with at that moment. He turned his squinty eyes on their uninvited guests. "All right, Agent Sympathy," Fearless Leader said smoothly. "We'll cooperate. We don't want anyone to be hurt, now, do we?"

But Karen didn't trust the beady-eyed foreign dictator. "Let me see your hands!" she shouted. "And whatever you're holding—drop it immediately!"

Fearless Leader smiled like a shark. "Gladly."

He raised his hands and dropped the remote control. As soon as it hit the floor, it turned on a whole bank of TV monitors. All were showing *Three Funny Wacky Spies & Their Horse, Who Will Also Be a Spy*.

Karen quickly turned away. "Don't look, Rocky! It's a trick. It'll turn you into a . . ." She looked at Rocky and gasped. The little gray squirrel had a dopey look on his face. He was staring at the TV screens.

Oh no. Too late!

Rocky was hypnotized!

Karen's tough FBI agent facade melted at the sight of her friend. The little girl inside her knelt beside him and took his face in her hands. "Rocky, Rocky . . ." she murmured.

But Rocky couldn't hear her. Even worse, Karen had let down her guard.

Boris and Natasha had a lot to make up for. They jumped at the opportunity to grab her.

Karen gasped and struggled in their clutches, but they held her tight.

"So, Agent Sympathy," Fearless Leader said, "you and the flying rodent have come to crash our little party . . . but now you will be our special guests."

Boris sneered. "Now we give you taste of Pottsylvanian hospitability."

"That's ability to put you in hospital, dollink," Natasha added.

Karen hung her head in shame. Once again, she'd made a horrible mess of things. Was this the end?

There was only one hope. One chance to defeat the enemy.

A six-foot-seven moose. Bullwinkle J. Moose. In other words—they didn't have a prayer.

Having managed to completely miss New York, Bullwinkle meanwhile, had flown instead to Washington, D.C.

He buzzed the city's famous landmarks: the Washington Monument . . . the Lincoln Memorial . . . the Capitol Building . . .

"Gee, New York sure has changed a lot since my day," Bullwinkle said. He had no idea he was in the wrong city. "Hey!" he said, looking down. "They even moved the White House here!"

With a shrug, Bullwinkle landed his plane in the one place that seemed familiar: on the White House lawn—nose first!

The plane was a wreck. But Bullwinkle was, after all, a cartoon. So he stepped out of the wreckage without a scratch. "Couldn't find the brakes," he muttered sheepishly.

He looked around. Hmm. No sign of Rocky or Karen. "Well, as long as I'm here, I might as well talk to the president about the trees!" With new determination, he headed for the steps of the White House.

Back in the RBTV studio, Rocky and Karen were now wearing protective glasses. They were shielded from the brain-numbing effects of RBTV's programming.

But they were handcuffed—prisoners of Fearless Leader!

Rocky struggled to get free, but it was no use. The real-life handcuffs held his cartoon wrists as tight as any drawn ones.

Fearless Leader grinned. If there was one thing he adored, it was a captive audience. He glanced at the clock. He had just enough time to brag to the squirrel and the girl about his sinister plan for world domination.

"Once I am president of the U.S.A., I will broadcast RBTV to all the nations of the world. Earth will become a planet full of mindless zombies, watching, watching, always watching. The whole world will be one big TV show. Starring me—Fearless Leader!"

On the TV screens behind him, the RBTV logo—a spinning Earth—turned into Fearless Leader's grinning head.

"As for you, my dear," he said to Karen, "we have planned something quite special."

He pressed a button on the wall, and an electric chair with a metal helmet rose from a trapdoor in the floor.

Beside it rose a kiddie high chair with its own helmet.

With great pleasure, Boris and Natasha strapped Karen into the big chair and Rocky into the high chair.

"We're hooking you directly to Quality Control," Fearless Leader explained pleasantly. "As soon as we go live, the current will pass through your brain and you will be turned into a mindless vegetable."

Karen wished she could reach out and hold Rocky's hand. "I'm sorry," she told him. "I've really done it this time."

But Rocky shook his head. "Don't worry, Karen. You need the most faith when things look the most hopeless."

"Yes, don't worry, Karen," Fearless Leader mocked. "It won't hurt. At least—I've never heard a complaint from the other vegetables!" He threw back his head and laughed.

On the other side of the studio, three human-sized vegetables dressed in suits and sunglasses and strapped in chairs popped up from the floor.

Fearless Leader smiled politely as if introducing guests at a party. "I think you recognize your three missing agents from the FBI?"

Karen stared in horror.

"Karen," Rocky said, "this is pretty hopeless."

Karen did indeed feel hopeless. But she tried to be strong. She tried to act tough. "Look, we don't care what you do to us . . . just leave America alone!"

Fearless Leader smirked. "Ah, America . . . well, as a matter-of-fact, there is another choice you can make, Agent Sympathy. A choice other than joining the salad bar. A choice that could turn you into a very important person in your beloved America . . . our beloved America." He stepped closer and stared into Karen's eyes.

Yuck, Karen thought. Is Fearless Leader . . . flirting with me?

"Come with me to Washington, Karen," Fearless Leader proposed. "They won't laugh at you or call you weak when you're at my side. In my new regime I will make you head of the FBI."

"Head of the FBI?" Karen breathed. Me? She couldn't help herself. It was a wonderful thought.

Fearless Leader saw the glint in her eye. "Join me," he urged her, his voice deep and hypnotic. "With your spirit and my evil genius, we could rule the world!"

Karen hesitated.

One word. That was all it would take to make her dreams come true.

The situation was hopeless, anyway. Wasn't it?

There was no way to stop Fearless Leader now.

Why not give up—and give in?

Fearless Leader looked deep into her eyes and smiled. "Well?"

CHAPTER 19

Ouch!

Karen felt the little girl inside her—the honest, innocent part of her— give her a swift kick.

It was just the jolt she needed to resist the devious dictator's slimy suggestions.

"Join you?" Karen exclaimed. "I wouldn't join you even if you turned me into a whole cabbage patch!"

Fearless Leader's smile vanished. He despised being disobeyed. Especially by a pretty girl. "Very well," he said in a cold, harsh voice. "You had your chance."

Karen raised her chin in defiance—and tried to keep it from trembling.

Beside her, Rocky whispered, "I'm proud of you."

Karen gave him a grateful smile.

It was all fine and good to stand up for one's

beliefs. But now Rocky would have to suffer too.

Boris put a helmet on Rocky. Natasha did the honors with Karen.

Then they attached them directly to Quality Control.

Fearless Leader sighed in regret, then reached for a giant knob on Quality Control. It's settings read:

Couch Potato
Mesmerized
Catatonic
Total Vegetation

With a shrug, he set the dial to Total Vegetation.

"Listen, Fearless Leader," Karen shouted at him, "if there's one thing this plucky squirrel has shown me, it's that you have to be who you are, no matter how much pressure there is to change!"

The little girl inside of Karen cheered.

But the entire nation was still poised on the brink of unimaginable doom. Fearless Leader's final election-grabbing broadcast was only minutes away. And there seemed to be no one—absolutely no one—remotely capable of stopping him.

Or was there?

CHAPTER 20

Bullwinkle was a moose with a mission. He strode down the hallway of the White House, looking for the Oval Office.

Heavens to Betsy, but the joint was quiet. Where was everybody?

"Hel-loooo, Mr. Pres-I-dent . . ."

Bullwinkle walked past some Secret Service men—men who had been hired to protect the president.

Did they stop and shout, "Who goes there?" Did they question a moose loose in the halls of the White House?

No. They didn't even look at him. They just stared at their TV, as still as two department store dummies.

"Next week," said the RBTV announcer, "on *Action Doctor Spies* . . ."

Bullwinkle was too busy to watch TV right now.

So he kept walking. "Yoo-hoo, Mr. President . . ."

He passed a secretary who had a tiny TV on her desk.

"Now back to our show," said the announcer. *"Three Funny Wacky Spies & Their Horse, Who Will Also Be a Spy."*

"But, Vladimir," said Spy #1, "the horse has swallowed the transmitter!"

"Not again!" said Spy #2.

Bullwinkle walked past the White House Mole. He stared stupidly at a portable Watchman TV. Even he was mesmerized.

Blissfully unaware, Bullwinkle kept looking. At last he found the president in the Oval Office, and he pleaded his case. . . .

"So you see, Mr. President, all the trees in Frostbite Falls are gone. The birds have no place to put their things. The children have no place to build their tree house. I built them a stump house, but they say it's just not the same. Please help when you have time." Bullwinkle stopped and waited politely for the president to say something.

But the president didn't say a word. He sat so still, he could have been a statue of the president. His eyes were glued to a desktop TV.

"They sure enjoy their TV at the White House," Bullwinkle said. He shrugged. Maybe he'd just wait till the show was over. Maybe then he would have the president's full attention.

Bullwinkle sat down and started to look at the president's show.

"Psst! Psst!" FBI Director Cappy Von Trappment hissed frantically at Bullwinkle from the next room. He was wearing sunglasses and soundproof earphones to protect himself from RBTV. He waved at Bullwinkle to follow him.

But Bullwinkle just stared at the TV.

"Oh, no!" Cappy cried. "Not you, too!"

"Not a bad show, eh, Mr. President?" Bullwinkle said.

Cappy's mouth dropped open. Bullwinkle was watching TV—but he wasn't hypnotized?

Yes, as cheap as it may seem—and it certainly does seem cheap—Bullwinkle's head was so thick that Fearless Leader's mind-numbing program had absolutely no effect on him whatsoever.

"At least one thing hasn't changed," Bullwinkle said. "TV is as good as ever."

Cappy rolled his eyes. "Come here!"

Bullwinkle walked over to join Cappy in the Oval Office's waiting room.

There was no TV in the small room, but there was a computer. Cappy took off his protective sunglasses and earphones. "Bullwinkle, allow me to be frank."

"Okay. Allow me to be Bullwinkle."

Cappy shook hands with the big moose.

"Cappy Von Trappment, FBI."

"I thought you said your name was Frank!"

"Shut up, Bullwinkle."

"Okay, Frank."

Cappy shook his head and continued. "As we speak, ninety-nine percent of America is slobbering in front of the television."

"What's so strange about that?" Bullwinkle asked.

Cappy sighed in exasperation. "Have you heard anything from Karen and Rocky?" he asked.

"Karen and Rocky?" Bullwinkle looked around, surprised. "You mean they're not here?"

"Of course not," said Cappy. "They're in New York."

Bullwinkle looked shocked. "I thought this was New York."

Cappy pointed toward the Oval Office. "No, Bullwinkle. That's Washington out there."

Bullwinkle thought he was pointing at the president. "Really? I always thought he'd look a lot older."

Cappy began to pace nervously. "We should have heard from Karen by now. I'm afraid she and Rocky are in terrible danger." He checked his watch. "It's no use. Fearless Leader's address starts in less than two minutes. There's no way anyone can get there in time now."

"Oh, butterballs!" Bullwinkle exclaimed. "If only there were some way of transmitting computer-generated animated characters across great distances in the blink of an eye."

Cappy's eyes lit up. He stared at the computer screen. "Bullwinkle! That's it!"

"It is?"

Cappy grabbed Bullwinkle's hand and pulled him to the computer. Quickly he typed in an E-mail address: fearlessleader@RBTV.com.

"Bullwinkle!" Cappy exclaimed. "We're going to E-mail you to New York!"

"Oh! You mean like when a car sticks its tongue out at you?"

"Exactly. Ready, hold on! One . . . two . . ." He grabbed Bullwinkle by the antlers and thrust him at the computer's disk drive.

"Three!" Bullwinkle said—just as Cappy shoved him into the disk drive.

The world seemed to rush past Bullwinkle in a whoosh!

Then he found himself inside the presidential computer.

Icons—little pictures—floated all around him.

"Look, Frank!" Bullwinkle exclaimed. "Solitaire!"

"We don't have time for that, Bullwinkle!" Cappy snapped. He moved the computer's mouse and clicked on Send.

As the crusty but warmhearted G-man hit the Send icon, our heroic moose grabbed the corners of the E-mail envelope and hung on for the ride of his life.

Back at the RBTV studio, Fearless Leader straightened his eye patch. Show time! he thought merrily.

Nearby, Boris and Natasha watched anxiously.

Strapped to Quality Control, Karen watched even more anxiously.

The deadly countdown began.

"Ten . . . nine . . . eight . . ." the floor director called out.

Little red lights on Karen's helmet began to blink.

"Seven . . . six . . ."

A shiver ran through her as she looked over at the three FBI vegetables.

We're next, she thought. Nothing can stop it from happening now.

CHAPTER 21

"Wa-hoo!" Bullwinkle got to his feet on the little picture of the E-mail envelope. He was surfing the Internet!

"Cowabunga!" he shouted. "I'm hangin' eight!" (Like lots of cartoon characters, Bullwinkle only had four toes on each foot.)

In what was a mere fraction of a second in the real world, Bullwinkle surfed past an awesome rush of images.

Millions of icons from millions of Web sites from around the world. Billions of E-mail letters. Music. Ad sites. Voices in every language.

Suddenly the RBTV Web site loomed before him like the Emerald City of Oz.

"Uh-oh. Wipeout!" Bullwinkle hung on to his envelope surfboard and rode it straight into the Web site.

Everything slowed down. Floating icons surrounded him.

Bullwinkle found himself inside the RBTV computer with only seconds left to spare.

And absolutely no idea how to get out.

"Five . . ." the floor director called out.

Karen was sitting not far from the RBTV computer. So she was the only one who heard a little voice inside the computer say, "You've got mail!"

Karen glanced at the screen—then did a double take.

Bullwinkle! He was only about an inch and a half tall, riding around the computer screen on a teeny, tiny envelope-shaped surfboard.

"Bullwinkle!" said Rocky. "Hurry up! Click on something!"

Bullwinkle looked around at his choices. "Mine Sweeper?"

"Print! Print!" Karen cried.

"Four . . ." the floor director called out, "three . . ."

Bullwinkle didn't see that the Print icon was right beside him. "Gee, it's all so confusing . . ."

Karen groaned.

Fearless Leader smiled for the camera.

"Two . . . one . . ."

The floor director gave Fearless Leader his cue.

"My fellow Americans," Fearless Leader began, "Say hello to your new Fearless Leader! Yes, you need me to run your country. You really need me."

Quality Control began to hum. The blinking red lights on Karen's and Rocky's headsets turned green. Green for go!

Zap! Rocky turned into a huge artichoke.

Zap! Karen turned into a giant tomato.

"But, Boris," Natasha whispered, "I thought tomato was fruit—"

"Yes," Boris whispered back, "but it thinks it's a vegetable."

"The polls are soon ready to open," Fearless Leader said into the TV cameras. "Go out and vote me in as your leader! Vote for Fearless Leader!"

Inside the RBTV computer, Bullwinkle sat down to think.

Lucky for him, he sat down right on top of the Print icon.

The printer hummed.

As Fearless Leader continued his speech, a pair of cartoon antlers slowly rose behind him from out of the printer. To those watching TV, it looked as if Fearless Leader were sprouting antlers.

The spies were shocked. The cameraman gasped. No one was quite sure what they were seeing.

Fearless Leader continued with his speech.

The studio technicians froze. They didn't know what to do.

"You Americans will submit to me!" Fearless Leader raved on. "You will bask in glory of all that is Pottsylvanian!"

Slowly, inch by inch, foot by foot, the rest of Bullwinkle—a full-sized Bullwinkle—flowed out of the printer.

Wow, what a weird trip that was! Bullwinkle shook his head.

And as he did, something strange happened.

Bullwinkle's mighty antlers jammed the Quality Control signal—reversing the vegetation process.

The tomato and the artichoke turned back into Karen and Rocky.

And all the TV monitors filled with snow.

Boris and Natasha watched in horror as Karen and Rocky yanked off their Quality Control headsets, leaped out of their chairs, and ran to join Bullwinkle.

"Boris!" Natasha cried. "Do something!"

"Bullwinkle!" Rocky said. "Am I glad to see you!"

"I don't know, Rock. Are you?"

Rocky laughed. "Of course I am!"

"All right!" Karen whooped. "We're a team again! Bullwinkle's back! "

"Yeah," Bullwinkle said, "and my front's here, too."

Rocky and Karen giggled. Same old Bullwinkle!

But then their reunion was cut short.

"Fearless Leader!" Boris shouted. "Moose is loose!"

Fearless Leader's head snapped around. When he saw our heroes reunited, he forgot all about being on television. He turned purple with rage. "Get them!" he screamed.

In a final, desperate measure, Boris tried one more time to master the technological complexities of the CDI computer.

He threw it at Bullwinkle's head!

Lucky for Bullwinkle, he missed.

Fearless Leader suddenly realized that he had totally lost it on national TV. Straightening his jacket, he turned back to the camera and smiled. "My first campaign promise is to rewrite the Constitution," he said in his hypnotic voice. "From now on, I am the Constitution. I am the government. I am the law! You will vote for Fearless Leader!"

Boris and Natasha, followed by a mob of Pottsylvanian spies, took off after Karen, Rocky, and Bullwinkle as Fearless Leader continued his speech.

They rushed Karen and grabbed her from both sides. But Karen vaulted off their shoulders, did an acrobatic flip, and clunked their heads together from behind. Boris and Natasha fell in an unconscious heap.

Bullwinkle was charged by a half dozen spies who piled up on him all at once. With expert head fakes, Bullwinkle managed to catch all six on his antlers. Then Bullwinkle shook them off, like a dog shaking off water. Spies went flying, smashing into TV monitors.

Then the moose charged Fearless Leader.

With his antlers, Bullwinkle flipped Fearless Leader, sending him up into the air.

The astonished dictator landed on Boris and Natasha.

Rocky flew in great, swift circles around Fearless Leader, Boris, and Natasha, wrapping them up with TV cable. For an added touch, he tied it up in a nice, neat bow.

Suddenly Bullwinkle realized he was standing right in front of the TV cameras. And they were on the air!

"Bullwinkle," Rocky whispered loudly. "Finish the speech!"

"Oh, okay." Bullwinkle cleared his throat and smiled at the camera. "My fellow . . ." He blinked. Then he hid his mouth behind his hand and whispered to Karen, "Forgot my line!"

"Just tell them to turn off the TV and vote for whoever they want," Rocky prompted.

Bullwinkle gave him a thumbs-up sign. Then he

smiled into the camera. "Turn off your TV and vote for whoever you want!"

Karen stuck her head into the shot to add, "And whoever wins the election, replant the forest at Frostbite Falls!"

And sure enough, all across America, something amazing happened.

RBTV viewers turned off their television sets and faced the difficult question of who they actually wanted to vote for. . . .

People in average American homes dug their newspapers out of the recycling bin and began to read about the candidates.

In sports bars and cafés, people began to debate issues with friends and neighbors.

In the White House, secretaries and doormen and Secret Service agents came out of their hypnotic trances.

In the Oval Office, the president woke up and turned off his TV. "Hmm," he said, stroking his chin. "Must do something about those trees. . . ."

Back in the RBTV studio, something else amazing happened. The Pottsylvanian spies cheered. They were so happy to be freed from Fearless Leader's iron-clad grasp, they made our heroes their heroes.

A party broke out. Confetti and balloons filled the air as the ex-spies danced around Fearless

Leader, Boris, and Natasha, who were still tied up in a bow.

Fearless Leader pouted. Natasha's mascara ran with her tears.

"I hate these happy endings," Boris grumbled.

Karen picked up the CDI from the floor. "Well, we won't be needing this anymore."

"Oh, that reminds me!" Bullwinkle said. "I should E-mail that nice Frank and thank him for all his help!" He grabbed the CDI computer from Karen and began to type on its keyboard.

"No!" everyone in the room shouted.

The beam shot out of the CDI. Everyone ducked as it bounced around the room. It was heading straight for Bullwinkle!

ZANGGGGG!

The beam hit Bullwinkle—right in the antlers. It ricocheted off them and zapped Fearless Leader, Boris, and Natasha.

Instantly they turned back into their cartoon forms. And the three villains were launched up into the stratus of the Internet, shot up at breakneck speed, and were launched skyward in a dazzling pyrotechnic display.

People on the street gaped in wonder as the three cartoons soared past.

"Aaaaaagh!"

* * *

Back in the studio, Karen made sure that no one would ever use the Quality Control machine again. She crashed a huge mallet down on top of the machine and smashed it to pieces.

Instantly the three vegetables from the FBI were transformed. The giant carrot, potato, and radish morphed into people who looked like a carrot, a potato, and a radish.

"Thanks, Agent Sympathy!" the three agents said.

And that was the end of Quality Control.

The very next day, in schools and community centers all across the country, Americans turned out in droves to cast their votes.

In the White House, President Signoff sat at his desk. And after hearing about a machine that could hypnotize voters, He made a solemn pledge to clean up the electoral process in the future. "This calls for a serious investigation," he said, winking at the camera.

Karen, Cappy, Rocky, and Bullwinkle walked along Washington D.C.'s Mall, the wide, grassy park in the heart of the city.

"Hey, if we fixed everything," Rocky said, "there's nothing left to do in the sequel to the movie!"

"With the jokes we've been telling," Bullwinkle

said, "I wouldn't worry about that, if I were you."

An agent, manager, and publicist swarmed around Bullwinkle.

"Never mind that, Bullwinkle, baby," the agent said. "There's always video and Europe."

"You're humongous in France," the manager said.

"Always a sign of class," Bullwinkle said.

Yes, Rocky and Bullwinkle were stars once again. Even Fearless Leader's old network, in a penny-pinching attempt to keep the same initials, changed its format from "Really Bad Television" to "Rocky and Bullwinkle TV."

"What's the difference?" Bullwinkle wondered.

Karen took Cappy aside. "Sir, there's one thing I still don't understand. Why did you pick me for this mission in the first place? I mean"—she looked down at her shoes, thinking of all her failures—"I'm clearly not FBI material."

But Cappy shook his head and raised Karen's chin with his finger. "FBI material is what gets the job done, Ms. Sympathy. If you needed an agent to work with a cartoon moose and squirrel, who would you send? Someone tough and hard-boiled? Or one of those annoying warmhearted, idealistic types?"

Karen grinned. So her boss had a soft spot in his heart after all! "Thank you, sir . . . I think," she said.

"Affirmative . . . Karen. Good work." For a second Karen thought her tough, gruff boss was actually going to smile. But then he turned, hitched up his pants, and walked off, hard-boiled as ever.

Karen turned back to Rocky and Bullwinkle. "Well . . . I really want to thank you guys for everything. And I really . . . Well, I'd really like to say . . ."

The voice of the little girl inside Karen knew what to say. It was as if she were talking through Karen.

"I'd . . . really like to say that I love you guys a lot." She smiled, then turned to go.

But the little girl inside her wasn't through. Karen turned back and said, "And if it hadn't been for you, I never would have learned . . . that hope and laughter are never out of date."

Bullwinkle was deeply moved. "And they say TV is shallow."

"Anyway," Karen said, "thanks for the adventure." She hesitated, embarrassed, then gave in to her true feelings and threw her arms around them. "So long."

She walked over to her car and got in.

"Where are you going?" Rocky asked.

Karen smiled a secret smile. "Um . . . the movies."

* * *

Back in Cow Tip, Oklahoma, the stars were coming out. It was a beautiful evening. Most folks had gone home for the night.

But not Ole, the prison guard. He was still waiting in front of the town's only movie theater for the girl of his dreams.

He'd grown a beard. He'd pitched a little tent. Tonight he sat in front of a little camping stove, making a hamburger and a pot of coffee.

It wasn't easy to keep waiting, but Ole was a patient guy. And after all, weren't the good things in life worth waiting for?

Suddenly he saw headlights coming down the road. His face lit up, and his heart leaped in his chest. Would this one slow down? Or drive on past, like all the others?

The car pulled to a stop. Ole rose to his feet and held his breath.

And then she stepped out.

"Hi," Karen said softly. "Sorry I'm late." She bit her lip and crossed her fingers behind her back and swore that this would be the last fib she would ever tell if she could just make everything turn out all right. "Couldn't find a parking space."

"Oh. That's okay," Ole said.

Shyly, Karen walked over and tried to take his hand. Only that was a bit of a problem since he was still holding a hamburger in one hand and a coffee cup in the other. But after a little juggling, they walked into the movie theater, hand in hand.

It was the late show, but better late than never.

Besides, they had been too busy looking at each other to read the name of the movie on the marquee:

NOW SHOWING—
VERY LIMITED ENGAGEMENT
THE ROCKY AND BULLWINKLE MOVIE
PRODUCED BY MINNIE MOGUL

And as Karen and Ole finally went to the movies, the president, back in the White House, made good on his posthypnotic suggestion. So in the middle of a beautifully restored forest just outside of town . . .

Yours truly, the Narrator, took a well-earned vacation, back where he knew he would always be welcome.

Mama's house.

Finally, all was well with our heroes.

Rocky was his old self again. . . .

"Ah, I'll never forget our trip to New York to visit President Washington," Bullwinkle said.

. . . and so was Bullwinkle.

About the Authors

Long before they met, Cathy East Dubowski and Mark Dubowski were fans of the original *Rocky and Bullwinkle* show. Now, just like that famous duo, the Dubowskis are a team. Together they have had many exciting adventures, including writing more than one hundred books for kids. Their book *Cave Boy,* which Mark also illustrated, received an International Reading Association/CBC Children's Choice award. They have also written the Rocky and Bullwinkle chapter book *Rocky and Bullwinkle and the Metal-Munching Mice.*

The Dubowskis each have their very own barn to write in behind their home in Chapel Hill, North Carolina. They live with their daughters, Lauren and Megan, and their two golden retrievers, Morgan and MacDougal.